Baroque-a-nova

A NOVEL BY

~~KEVIN CHONG~~

Kevin Chong

Penguin Books

PENGUIN BOOKS

Published by the Penguin Group

Penguin Books Canada Ltd, 10 Alcorn Avenue, Toronto, Ontario,
Canada M4V 3B2

Penguin Books Ltd, 27 Wrights Lane, London W8 5TZ, England

Penguin Putnam Inc., 375 Hudson Street, New York, New York 10014,
U.S.A.

Penguin Books Australia Ltd, Ringwood, Victoria, Australia

Penguin Books (NZ) Ltd, cnr Rosedale and Airborne Roads, Albany,
Auckland 1310, New Zealand

Penguin Books Ltd, Registered Offices: Harmondsworth, Middlesex,
England

First published 2001

1 3 5 7 9 10 8 6 4 2

*Publisher's note: This book is a work of fiction. Names, characters, places
and incidents either are the product of the author's imagination or are used
fictitiously, and any resemblance to actual persons living or dead, events,
or locales is entirely coincidental.*

Manufactured in Canada

Text design and typesetting by Ruthe Swern

CANADIAN CATALOGUING IN PUBLICATION DATA

Chong, Kevin
Baroque-a-nova

ISBN 0-14-100025-2

I. Title.
PS8555.H644B37 2001   C813'.6   C00-932483-6
PR9199.3.C46B37 2001

Visit Penguin Canada's website at www.penguin.ca.

This book is dedicated to my parents.

There is no moment that exceeds in beauty that moment when one looks at a woman and finds that she is looking at you in the same way that you are looking at her. The moment in which she bestows that look that says, "Proceed with your evil plan, sumbitch."

—Donald Barthelme, "The Sea of Hesitation"

Baroque-a-nova

Monday

Helena St. Pierre died one Monday. She was my estranged
mother, a long-ago radio siren. I was eighteen, slack-
jawed and gangly in army-surplus apparel, with narrow,
miserly eyes and greasy hair falling in them, heavy and frizzy
like wet yarn. I dressed like a badass, a surly malcontent: I
wore sixteen-holed combat boots, dark jeans, and a dull-
green button-up shirt, a tiny East German flag patched to its
right upper sleeve. Yet I couldn't grow a mustache if the fate
of nations rested upon it. I was counting away the seconds of
my last year of high school, of my last month, and while I
didn't learn about it until later, I was at school, in class staring at a metric ruler and sizing myself in millimeters, when
she killed herself seventeen time zones away.

I was cranky. I came from a family of cranks; that was how
I was made. I was the only native kid in school, half-blooded
or otherwise, the only kid whose father had long hair and
didn't hold a regular job, whose mother had run out under

mysterious circumstances. We lived in a semirural area; this was not even a real suburb. I was used to getting the crap kicked out of me. It was right before lunch and I felt, then and there, an overwhelming sense of structure.

Theories had arisen to explain my apathy. My best friend, Navi, a young revolutionary, suspected I had fallen victim to the alienating effects of a market economy. My father spoke up from his recliner and said I was lazy. My stepmother eyed me nervously from the kitchen sink, thinking I might have a learning disability. My friend Rose said I was nihilistic. For a term in her AP lit class, she read Russian novels: she quoted Maxim Gorky, who wrote in one of his suicide notes of a toothache in his heart.

They were all wrong. All I knew was that I felt adrift in longing, marshy and ungratified, in the smell of suntan lotion on freckled female shoulders. I felt dizzy with desire.

I was sad to the point of distraction.

Mr. Henry, our English teacher, had gone without coffee today. He took stubby strides into class, stifling a yawn as he wheeled a television and VCR to the front of the classroom, beside the yellowing poster of Knut Hamsun and a jade-leaf plant potted in a blue glazed vase. I was in English 12 again, where we were to be discussing a book I hadn't read because reading left so little time for important thoughts and activities. I had also lost my copy.

"Are we watching a movie?" I asked.

"Yes, Saul."

"I don't see any point."

"What are you getting at?"

"How does this film stimulate our critical thinking abilities?"

"Right, I know how much you care about critical thinking."

Mr. Henry stepped back and looked at me, his chin swallowed by doughy flesh. He was in his forties, a not-so-tall, round man with a mustache. He chewed toothpicks while marking papers and decorated his desk with model airplanes. I couldn't tell whether Mr. Henry loathed me or liked me. He dealt with every student in the same offhand manner, with condescension and slight disapproval. And when he was bored with certain assigned texts, at certain times in the school year, he would allow certain loudmouth students to fill up the class hour. I always stepped up, prompted by the very same tedium.

The class was silent; they waited for Mr. Henry to explode. The copies of our book, lugged here for no apparent reason, sat on their desks, their glossy paperback covers reflecting against fluorescent classroom lights. A book-banning felt so small-town, so feeble-minded, and it was only appropriate that my own school would so quickly pull it from our shelves, because no one wanted the trouble. I felt indignation welling inside me, struggling against my own natural apathy. Now I wished I had read the book, if only for the outrage it would have entitled me to.

"Have you given up on us already?" I asked.

"Some of you."

The class laughed. I raised my hand again.

"What about the book?"

"It's been pulled from the syllabus, Saul."

"Why?"

"Why? Because there have been complaints."

"Threats?"

"We don't want to take any chances."

"And how do you feel about that, Mr. Henry?"

"Hm. Well," Mr. Henry said, considering it, "not a whole lot. I would think you'd be one of the happier students, seeing the level of enthusiasm you've displayed for the assigned text over the past week. Have you even cracked it open?"

The room tittered. Some of my classmates—Mindy, the girl from the religious family who wore discarded nursing-school slacks, and Tony, who had white scars across his wrists—exchanged glances, rolled eyes and pimply frowns, but they fell in the minority, among the scorned. A girl sitting in front of me, Nancy, the one with the big head of amber highlights, turned around and caught me with the corner of her eye, her mouth turned in a faint smile. I felt encouraged to go on.

"This is shit."

Mr. Henry yawned, cupping his mouth with a closed fist, his face almost catlike. "Please watch the language, Saul."

"Precisely. Language is the issue. Freedom of expression."

"All right, Saul, that's enough."

Usually this signaled an end to Mr. Henry's patience. With his amusement waning, we were to return to our studies, but I wasn't prepared to give it a rest.

"These days you need to resort to vulgarity to be heard," I said. "You have to bring the violence home. You're a child of the sixties: I'd think you'd understand."

He raised an eyebrow and leaned back against his desk.

"What are you saying?"

"If I were to call the school and make an obscene threat, maybe then people would listen."

Mr. Henry snickered. He turned off the lights in the room,

casting our faces in the blue glow of the screen. Then he held up two cassette tapes.

"What will it be?" he asked the class. "*The Sweet Hereafter* or *The Handmaid's Tale?*"

"I hope you understand that I must leave this class in protest."

Mr. Henry sighed. He would have to report my absence, and I would end up in the principal's office again.

"Oh, Saul. Grow up."

I left class, found Rose in the library and convinced her to leave early. Rose couldn't say no to me. Fortunately, she was the only one who suffered from such a tragic affliction. Her parents worked during the day, so we went back to her house, ate some tiny microwave pizzas in front of the TV, removed our clothes and had maybe two and a half hot minutes of sex. Rose and I had had relations, as my stepmother liked to call it, for the first time a month ago, shortly after she'd recovered from mono. We were in my dad's car by the beach, underneath a gray sleeping bag.

Rose stood on the balls of her feet, flossing in front of her bathroom mirror. What can I say about Rose? She was about average height and wore her brown hair down to her shoulders. She had olive skin and incredible eyebrows. She was sweet-tempered and kind.

She was a dental-hygiene freak.

She flossed meticulously and exactly, as though each tooth were a tiny precious stone. Flossing was a function of her obsessiveness, especially now that we had started "having a relationship." Lately, she'd been acting paranoid, guilty, as though we'd

stolen something valuable and had tripped a silent alarm in our
escape. Our conversations now involved hours of nagging. Nights
of nagging. Nag-o-ramas. I started thinking of our arguments col-
lectively as Nagtoberfest. First, I was roundly chastised for being
withdrawn and sullen, for appearing at her house late at night,
asking to be let in through the back door and making her lie to
her parents, who hated me. Then she said I was shallow. Me. We
had been friends since sixth grade, but not once had I thought of
her in a romantic way, not one platonic kiss on her cheek, until
she got sick and lost all that weight. She was putting it back on
now, her face filling out and her belly showing, white, rippled and
squishy, and this was making her irritable.

Her mouth was twisted and drool ran down her chin. She
noticed me and threw her floss into the waste basket. Nagtime.

"I think we should reconsider our relationship," Rose said,
wiping her chin with Kleenex, then scrubbing her hands under
the tap.

"What do you mean?"

"My parents know about us."

"No, they don't."

"They do. They see you standing between me and the
accredited postsecondary institution of my choice."

I paused, putting on a wounded expression. "Your parents
should quit smoking crack," I sneered.

"My parents are not on crack," Rose said, suddenly sounding
hurt.

Her parents were environmental rights lawyers who made
sandwiches with pesto. Of course, I'm one to talk about weirdo
parents, with such lunacy in my family. But at least my dad—for
all his many, many faults—had a sense of humor. Rose certainly

didn't, and now it seemed like she might start crying, her eyes welling up the way a glass of milk rises to the brim and teeters there. In Science 10, we had learned a scientific word for when that happens, and I sat on her bed trying to remember it.

Then I wondered how quickly I could make it home.

I got dressed and went to the kitchen. In spite of the pizza we'd just had, I felt hungry, as though I could eat dog food if the situation got desperate, and began looking for something to gnaw on. I had excellent foraging skills, as I was always hungry and had access to strangers' kitchens. There were potato-and-onion perogies in the freezer. I set about cooking them, scraping burnt chili from a pot in the sink and filling it with water. I put the pot on the stove, let it heat, then added the perogies.

Rose sat down at the kitchen table.

I held up the bag of perogies. She shook her head.

"I'm not hungry."

The perogies started to float in the bubbling water. I normally liked to serve them with fried onions but was too hungry for anything remotely ambitious. I drained the perogies and put them on a plate; they were lumpy and white wedge-shaped things, like newborn strudels. One piece stuck to the bottom of the pot, so I used a plastic stirring spoon from the draining board to pry it loose.

"I should go to my dad's after I eat," I said. "The school has probably called him."

"Sure," Rose said. "Whatever you say."

I asked her where her parents kept the cutlery.

"Let me get it for you," she said, moving to a drawer. She cleared one half of the table, cluttered with newspapers and lawyer-type newsletters, and placed the knife and fork neatly in front of me. Then she stepped back to the counter and watched me eat. There was a look on her face, a look I've seen on my stepmother when she talks about my father, a stunned, heartstruck expression. So this was how you do it, I thought, stuffing perogies into my mouth. Without trying.

She picked up the napkin dispenser from the counter and set it down straight in front of me, between us.

"Here," she said. "Talk to this."

My father had an entire house to himself, a one-story painted a thoughtful, nursery-school blue, with a flat roof and a carport, on a street lined with modest houses, bric-a-brac homes with gnomic statuary and fussy latticed gardens. His house was part of a cul-de-sac at the end of the street. After the last St. Pierres concert, Dad retired here in the older part of our town, a suburb on the West Coast. This was where I grew up, with him and my stepmother, Jana, the woman who had raised me since I was a four-year-old.

Long ago, my parents made up a musical duo, the St. Pierres, my mother, the singer, and my father, the guitarist and principal songwriter. Their genius lay in flimsy balladry, schmaltz, and they found success in the seventies churning out folk rock, mid-tempo and sad, with occasional orchestral flourishes. They were like so many other singer-songwriters of that period, right before disco and punk crowded them off the airwaves. Until recently, none of my friends had even heard their music, its honky electric piano and treacly arrangements, those dated wah-wahs and synths on the last two albums. Then a German band named Urethra Franklin remade one of their songs into a

top-forty hit, sampling the chorus to "Bushmills Threnody." I'd
been hearing her voice a lot in the past few weeks. People said
my mother had run away, at least that was how my father put
it. I pictured a woman floating down a river in a barge, holding
a bundle and stick over her shoulder.

I wanted to run away, too.

Instead, I was living with my stepmother. In recent months,
visits to my father had come irregularly, usually when I wanted
money or needed permission slips signed. According to the
law, Dad was still my legal guardian. I was hoping to mention
today's incident before the school called him. What upset me
was the thought that they might ask him to school and that he
would fail to appear, as he had the last two times, not remem-
bering the appointment or not caring enough to show. I figured I should have a word with him about fecklessness, about
direction and responsibility.

I stepped through the front hallway, not bothering to take
off my boots, and into the narrow kitchen. The sink window
allowed a dusty light in the afternoon. The entire kitchen was
under renovation: the cabinets gutted, the floors ripped up, a
piece of tarp covering a hole in the ceiling. Last month, on one
of the few sunny days that May, Dad talked about a glassed-in
porch, a real yuppie add-on. I was surprised that though he
eventually decided against it, he had started the project. It was
something my stepmom had wanted done a couple of years
back when they were still together. "It's costing me ten thousand dollars," he would say. "Ten thousand dollars"—his avari-
cious refrain.

The living room was paneled, and included a small coffee
table and a fireplace. The carpet was thick and shaggy, patterned

in a gray-black-blue marble swirl. A set of *World Book* encyclopedias and Dad's dubbed movie collection—all Westerns—took
up an entire wall. When Jana left, she'd stripped the place bare
of its knickknacks, like the commemorative plates that weren't
for eating from or the colorful throws that had once covered the
couches but now seemed out of place, unsettled like confused
pets, on her new furniture. I expected to see Dad here, bare-
chested in a pair of shorts, high or drunk, watching afternoon
television—no doubt the cooking channel. I expected to see
him scratching his stomach, his eyes bloodshot and narrow. I
expected him to sigh when I walked in.

Instead there was a young woman, someone I didn't know, sitting on the couch where he should have been. She was in her
twenties, a blonde with thin eyebrows, wearing a white tank top,
pyjama bottoms and flip-flops. She was watching television.

"You're Saul, right?"

She offered her hand daintily, fingers scraping across my
palm.

Her name was Marina.

"I'm a friend of your dad's, I guess. From out of town."

"Since when?"

"Pretty recently."

"You're staying with him?"

"For a while," she said.

She flashed her bottom row of teeth. Then she looked
toward the ground and began to bite her thumbnail. She sat on
the black leather loveseat my stepmother had bought at a
fancy secondhand shop in the city. It was placed between a
banged-up recliner and a bentwood armchair. Her knees were
in the air, and she looked pretty brilliant in a tank top—I tend

to notice these things—her features finely cut and expressive.
She seemed foreign, a woman with a story, like a Denny's host-
ess who was once a star of television and cinema in a former
satellite country, a nation pocked with creaky nuclear reactors.
I focused on her feet, her toenails painted green, and thought
how perfect they were, her thin ankles held together as if by a
loose, invisible knot. She looked good.

"How long are you visiting?" I asked.

She yawned, her head falling back on her shoulders.

"Don't know. Week, maybe two. I'm here with my friend
Louise. She and I aren't on much of a schedule."

I was intrigued by the thought of two women.

"Where's Louise?"

"She's in the guest room."

"Where's my old man?"

"Out for the afternoon running errands, filling the propane
tank for the grill. He's having a barbecue tonight. You coming?"

I leaned back into the recliner and turned on the TV.

"I guess."

"Shouldn't you be at school?" she asked.

"School sucks." I spat this out with as much nonchalance as
I could manage, as if I were presenting my library card.

She bobbed her head in a friendly, ingratiating way.

"I finished my degree in communications last May. Wrote my
thesis on the female gaze in televised women's golf. I wouldn't
recommend college. Though, I don't know, maybe you'll like it
more. Your situation might be different. With me, it was all
about normalizing."

"Normalizing?"

"Academia is the culture of normalization."

"Oh."

"You can say I've had enough school."

"How do you know my dad?"

"Louise and I wrote him a fan letter."

I sat down on Dad's squishy couch, stunned. From there, I picked up an issue of *Maclean's* from January 1994 on the coffee table, put it down, then tried to make sense of things. I wondered whether my dad had had his way with Marina. The thought didn't sit so well.

Another woman appeared by the kitchen entrance, carrying a laptop computer. Her face was tiny and pretty, her eyes crinkled toward one another.

Marina introduced Louise.

"I'm making coffee," Louise said. She smiled nervously, then set off.

She placed her laptop on the coffee table, then disappeared into the kitchen. She had lovely arms. And she really did have a pretty face, although her hair looked as if it had been dyed one too many times, and now had the same color as a cup of tea made from a bag that has been reused.

"We corresponded," Marina said. "Three letters, one phone call. I sent him a photo, a picture of the two of us after we'd played tennis, you know, to show that we were sporty. We decided to travel this summer. Both of us had a little cash pocketed, so we went west. First we took one long train down to New Mexico and hung around with my mom and her, like, sixteenth husband. Two weeks ago we ended up on a bus to Portland, just five hours south, because we'd heard good things about it." Marina made a sour face. "We thought it would be fun to come up. Ian said he'd pick us up on Friday, at that town right before the border. What's it called—Blaine? Sounds about right."

Louise came back into the living room and sat next to Marina. She held a Scotiabank mug and started tapping away at her laptop. "You look puzzled, Saul," Louise said.

"I guess I am."

"Well, come on. Spill the beans."

"My dad's not rich, you know." This was true. My father blamed the government for the fact that he wasn't wealthy. There were layabouts, he complained, getting free chiropractic and mammograms off his sweat. Still, for someone so concerned about money, he never worked. Mostly he puttered and drank. He phoned his lawyer to check whether any intellectual property had recently been stolen—no such luck. He went to the public library to send abusive e-mail to his stockbroker, whose advice he had taken on bad oil investments. "I mean, if you think he's rich, then you're completely off base."

Marina scanned the living room. "You don't say."

"Then what's the big deal about my old man?"

"Saul," Louise said, her eyes bulging, "your father's a fricking genius. There are these things on that album, little sounds that come out of the left speaker that you can't hear without a good set of headphones: Tibetan percussion, telephones ringing. He single-handedly revitalized the glockenspiel in pop music. No one used glockenspiels before your father; now it's an industry standard. Everyone focuses on Helena St. Pierre, on her voice—you know, conceptual artist, oppressed person, blah, blah, blah—but they don't really understand that Ian provided the substance in the band. His music is sensitive, yet masculine."

"His music," Marina said, "makes me feel among people."

Louise looked at her and nodded. "He's like the Toshiro Mifune of pop music."

We were watching the French-language music channel, which was exactly like the English-language music channel, only with pouty Québécois VJs who all seemed to be wearing clamdiggers that summer. I wondered whether my father really was that famous, worthy of attention from strange, young female admirers. Maybe it was Urethra Franklin that brought their attention to my father. Because of them his music had been in the news recently: I had been watching the French-language channel last night at Rose's when they aired an interview and a clip of the band performing their "Bushmills" cover, fast gaining popularity in North America. The keyboardist spoke about listening to smuggled St. Pierres records when he was growing up in Communist East Germany. He went on about my Indian mother, a woman who had disappeared from the public almost twenty years ago, and the beauty of the native people. Then they showed another clip, one from the coming-of-age gangster comedy that featured the song on its soundtrack.

Dad had griped only a month ago about how little money he was getting from the group, compared to what they were making from his song. He said he intended to change lawyers over it. I supposed there were other benefits to be had from this renewed interest.

I gave Marina the eye.

"Any plans while you're here?" I asked.

"What do you have in mind?" Marina said.

"There's a waterpark down the highway. A ten-minute

drive." I pointed out the window. "You can actually see it from the backyard."

"Is it much fun?"

"It's mostly for the under-twelve set," I said, "but bigger people are allowed."

"*Bigger* people."

"Whatever," I said, flustered. My face felt warm.

She smiled radiantly.

"Louise has your dad's biography, one written by a puffy-faced fellow. The author's face takes up the whole back cover."

"Erickson," Louise said. "I found it at a used bookstore for twenty-five cents. It was in a barrel."

"I know people who work there," I said, "and they have staff keg parties the last Thursday of the month—if you're going to be here that long."

"One with a picture of you on a sled, with you all tiny."

"*Adorable*," Marina said.

"Oh." I remembered that picture. "That must've been taken—probably at my grandparents', who lived in northern Ontario."

"You look like your dad," Marina said.

"Fine. No waterslides."

"His eyes. Those gorgeous eyes."

I had his eyes, which were narrow and gray, and his Hungarian count eyebrows, which flared out toward his temples. I had his bony hands and his rounded shoulders. I would probably inherit his stocky midsection. We walked the same way, sort of bowlegged and slouched, and we sounded alike when we answered the phone—groggy and impatient and needy all at the same time, an emotional boilermaker. I wondered when this had taken place, under my nose, how I'd turned into my father. It must have happened in my sleep.

"But you have your mother's coloring. Her native-American cheekbones."

"So you're here you don't know how long?"

"Precisely," Marina said.

I went home to Jana's, taking the pedestrian overpass that stretches above the highway. I lived in a flat, drained municipality thirty minutes south of Vancouver whose outskirts were populated by faded barns and electrical towers. It was early in June. The weather was warm and clear, breezy, a welcome change from April and early May, when it had been gray and wet. From the overpass I could see traffic wash in from the city along Highway 17 past the intersection, the hockey and curling rink, the cow pastures where new housing developments were planned, the highway stretching toward Tsawwassen and the ferry to Vancouver Island. We were right by the ocean. I stood over rumbling cars at the intersection: sedans pulling motorboats, green Celicas and baby-blue Accords driven by men in suits—sunglasses installed on their prescription eyewear and parking stubs collecting on their dashboards—trucks with cabs, a Volkswagen Passat driven by two women in saris, a BMW with a body-board on its roof, a junky Datsun rusted the color of a nosebleed.

Drivers could read about Marcel and Ivy's twentieth anniversary. Or the hockey team. People hung signs from the Day-Glo green overpass railing, bed sheets spray-painted with endearments. Up ahead, the highway was being repaved. I saw a woman in an orange vest directing drivers to one lane.

Two fire engines crossed Highway 17 into town, their sirens ornery, followed by a pair of police cars.

An old Chinese woman sat at the bus stop in a floppy garden hat, her feet not touching the ground.

Here trees stood tall and narrow, planted in rows to prevent soil erosion.

I spat on a Chevy Nova.

The further east you went, the newer the houses were. Navi lived in the housing development beside the overpass, a giant gray house with darker gray trim that fit at least thirteen people and a Steinway played by his brother, an eleven-year-old prodigy, among other boxy houses in cul-de-sacs. My stepmother's townhouse was just beyond. These homes had appeared only in the last ten years or so. I remembered playing baseball long ago where Navi lived, when it was an empty lot, but now the area was overrun with homes, housing mostly Indian families. Sikhs. Men with turbans and beards. Women traveling in pairs, in orange, beet and yellow gold-flecked fabrics. They kept their lawns trim and undecorated. They took up about two-thirds of the high school. An Indian veteran had not been allowed to enter the local legion hall on Remembrance Day because he was wearing a turban, and headwear was forbidden. It had gotten into the newspapers and our homely little suburb was declared the hate capital of the province.

I leaned forward against the railing, as far as I could stomach, until I was almost horizontal. I watched the old woman at the bus stop watch me, disapproving, then finally uninterested.

I wanted to leave.

The landscape, the flatness, the low-slung buildings.

I spat on a blue Honda Civic.

My stepmother, Jana, was dressed to go out, in a satin blouse and a string of pearls across her neck, as she carried a basket of dirty laundry to the closet facing the stairs, where the washer-dryer was located. We lived in a townhouse complex, a collection of narrow salmon-colored buildings encircling a parking lot and the grassy, shrubbed median at its center like a bull's-eye. The development was quiet, especially during the day. Its residents were either retirees and divorcees like my stepmother, who worked as an office temp, or young professional couples, accountants and lawyers intent on owning a home—people on their way up, or on their way down. There weren't any children here. No one, it seemed, went to the trouble.

"You're supposed to be at the principal's office at quarter to nine."

A school secretary had phoned.

"Since when does the school call you?" I asked.

"Your father referred them to me after your last final warning." Jana shrugged, placing the basket on the dryer and pulling out the whites from the rest of the clothes. "He says he hardly sees you, anyway."

"I bet he's crying buckets."

"Where were you today, if you don't mind me asking?" she said. This was the way she asked questions—casually and off the beat.

I mentioned Rose and Dad, but left out his two visitors.

"How is Rose?"

"Studying, as usual."

"And is she feeling better? She's gotten so thin."

"She's getting heavier," I said.

"Oh. Well, that's good."

"She's turning into a whale."

"*Saul*, that's not nice."

I grunted, then went to the kitchen. Jana dumped towels and underwear into the washer, dousing them with a capful of blue liquid detergent, and then closed the machine's lid.

Jana was from Cape Breton. She was short. She had thick hips and round cartoon eyes and was the most important person in my life. She followed me into the kitchen, where I found a cold cinnamon roll in the refrigerator and gobbled that down even though it was stale. I raised my eyes from the bun and looked at Jana. I thought she looked tired, her eyes puffy. She approached, placed a hand on my hip and brushed my nose with her finger.

"You eat too much. Someday you'll have to pay for it. You'll pay through the nose."

"I'll find union work," I said. "I'm young; I'm eager. I'll go into forestry."

"I'm glad you have your life all mapped out."

"Oh, you know"—I smiled, swatting my hand at her playfully—"I had a couple of hours free last night."

"And your father? How is he?"

"Same old, I guess."

"Hm. Same old something."

"He's renovating the kitchen."

"Well, la-di-da."

"La-di-da," I repeated.

"I have a date tonight."

"Officer Dale?"

"Mm-hm. We're going to sing karaoke at the Silver and Gold."

You're so lame, I thought, feeling shame surge across my face. Out of guilt, I offered to vacuum the house.

"As you may recall, I did that yesterday. But thank you, thank you for your hollow and, no doubt, limited-time offer." She went into the bathroom to put on earrings, walking the mannish way she did when hurrying, shoulders forward, hands in fists. "I'd appreciate it if you could fix your own dinner."

"I'm going to Dad's."

"Since when does he have you over for dinner?"

"Since now, I suppose."

Jana grunted like she was amused, but really wasn't.

"Well, isn't he one for surprises?"

She stepped out of the bathroom, clicking off the light, found her purse on the kitchen counter, took out a pack of cigarettes and lit one.

"Dale better not be late tonight. I swear."

My father had been a chain-smoker until he stopped cold turkey last year, just to see if he could. Dad could do things like that. He thought it silly that others couldn't break habits as easily. He called it self-discipline—I sort of thought it a result of being such a hopeless strap-on. Jana had no such willpower. Even though she'd once told me she smoked only because of being around Dad, that she'd quit now that they were separated, there she was, puffing away.

I went to my room upstairs and lay on my bed reading comics, before turning on the radio. First the top-forty station and then the college station were playing "Bushmills

Threnody," the German remix, which featured electronic dance sounds, spacey pulses and my mother's sampled voice, over which the lead singer of Urethra Franklin rapped in brutal, politicized English.

The phone rang. Rose wanted to know whether I had heard about the toxic nerve gas.

"What?"

Somebody had called in a threat at school. Students were moved away, gathered on the soccer field, where they milled around nervously, discussing what was the year of *Anschluss*, movie adaptation versus comic book versus video game. They talked about *Star Wars* and Spice Girls and the chicks at school with the fattest asses. They sat on the grass watching a couple of guys try to hacky-sack a green apple. A lonely girl sat alone with her guitar, strumming listlessly.

They watched the Dumpster being searched. Policemen stood around. Experts, presumably, were consulted.

I figured some kid didn't want to write a chemistry exam. I thought it was funny, but Rose insisted it was no joke.

"It was on the news at six. Weren't you tuned in?"

Rose's family would eat dinner together with the news on. They would then retire to the living room, whereupon they would hold forth, like a panel discussion group, on the greater world at hand, a topic that led to endless discomfort for me whenever I was invited for dinner.

The door slammed downstairs. From the window in my room, I watched Jana step into Officer Dale's truck in the early evening light. He was holding the car door, and her shoulders bent in deference to him, bearing the weight of his shadow. Officer Dale had a fire hydrant for a neck, a face all pink and sweaty, and an open yard of crew-cut blond hair. As a way of gaining my approval, he'd once let me try out his handcuffs, so I thought he was cool enough, even if he was a cop and his verbal skills weren't too great. Jana liked him, I could tell, because of the way she glanced at him, quickly, as if he were something that must be taken sparingly.

"You should really keep abreast of current events, Saul."

"I don't get the news."

There was a car in Dad's driveway next to his Volkswagen Jetta, a truck belonging to his friend Gord. Gord owned a contracting business. Painted on the side of his truck was the company's logo—a cartoon caricature of a lanky hippie guy, deceptively docile and ingratiating, with nails in his mouth, swinging a hammer in the air. I slipped the latch and opened the back-fence gate. Even for the yards in this neighborhood, my father's was large, with yellow patchy grass—a neighbor's dog snuck in through a hole in the fence to pee—and an unpainted picnic table. At the very end, beside a small fir tree, was a white toolshed where he kept a manual lawn mower. Past it, empty fields, then the highway. Dad was at the grill, Marina and the Coburns, Gord and Nadine at the picnic table. Louise sat on a stool next to Dad.

Stuck to the barbecue was a blob of green plastic and bristle —a brush that had been left too close to the grill and melted onto its side like a squashed caterpillar. Dad stood looking over a set of ribs and some chicken wings. He took my hand and pulled me toward him, swinging his other arm, one with a pair of kitchen tongs, over my shoulder loosely into an awkward embrace.

"Why haven't you called?" he asked, returning to the ribs.

"I didn't know I was supposed to."

"I haven't seen you in weeks."

"Keeping busy."

"Oh, well. Good."

We didn't have much to say, never had.

Dad wiped his eyes using his wrists.

"Don't these look good?" he said, nodding at the ribs.

"As usual."

"We'll eat well."

His tangly, Summer of Love hair had been let down and fell to his shoulders, and he had shaved off his beard, which he'd worn carelessly for the past two or three months. He seemed healthier than the last time I saw him, his belly stretching against a faded blue T-shirt. His legs were still pale and pasty in those camouflage shorts he found at an army-surplus sale I took him to, but there was a smile on his round face, his eyes, my eyes, squinting and gleaming. Good for him, I thought. Maybe he was getting laid; maybe that would turn him around.

Gord had a pair of chicken wings in his mouth. Long ago he had been Dad's pedal-steel player, the longest-serving member of the St. Pierres' touring band and Jana's old boyfriend. He was an inveterate pot smoker, six feet six inches tall, in jeans and a Winnipeg Jets jersey, with a long face and white hair that ran down his back. After the band's demise, he started his own contracting business, doing small construction jobs and renovations, which presently included Dad's kitchen. "Ten thousand dollars," Gord once huffed when Ian complained. "He doesn't know how cheap he's getting it." Nadine was his obnoxious young wife, maybe only a few years older than Dad's visitors. She was heavily made up, in hot pants and a belly shirt, her hair held back with a banana clip. She reminded me of a hamster. Her eyes were small and dark, and when you looked directly at her, her nose wrinkled.

Marina was still wearing her flip-flops. Gold-rimmed aviator specs sat atop her head in the accessorized way women wear sunglasses. She was drinking sangria from a green plastic jug with a wooden spoon in it. She raised her face when she saw me approaching, her eyes alighting on me slowly, and smiled upon recognition. I sat next to her.

"Let me pour you a glass, okay?" she said.

She took a plastic cup and filled it halfway and then scooped in pieces of fruit. It tasted strong, heavy on sherry and a little vinegary.

Louise was talking. She wasn't really American, she was saying, but a student from Toronto, working toward a library science degree at Columbia University.

"The library science is really a fallback," she said, smiling apologetically.

"Louise is working on a screenplay," Marina said. "But now she's hit a rut."

"The problem lies in the second act. You come up with a great idea, great characters, great situations. And you know how you want to end it. Character X finds true love, then dies. But between all that you need so much relevant action."

"Louise is writing a feminist tragedy that might possibly include figure skating," Marina said. "Sparkling dialogue. Arresting social themes touched."

"You need to cook up subplots, leitmotifs that are rich in association. Thread them together."

"Louise is hard on herself. We're working on that."

"It's not as easy as it might sound. All the narrative strands don't exactly meet at the end."

"It was going to be a novel, but she's come to realize where her strength lies—in imagery."

"It's loosely based on the life of Margaret Trudeau Kemper," Louise said glumly. "Possibly with figure skating."

"It's not as stupid as she makes it out to be."

"How did the two of you get the summer off to travel?" Gord asked.

"Well," Louise said, "as I was telling Ian, our sublet expired in May. We had a deal on the place, a two-bedroom with a view. A French architect uses it in the summer—Henri, who designs airport terminals—and lets it out to young women as his way of supporting his labor-friendly ideals. We met him once."

Marina laughed through her nose. "He walked in unannounced," she said, "get this, wearing dark glasses and a black skullcap, like a longshoreman. He said work had let out two weeks early for him and that we all had to make like good friends. The story goes he always surprises his female sublettors. He walks around the house in Speedos. A forty-five-year-old lech who listens to hip hop, who brought out a camera and said if we posed nude for him we could *reclaim* pornography. A real zeitgeist-monger, he is."

"You're the one who slept with him," Louise said. "May I add?"

"Okay, so what? There was nothing good on TV. The point remains."

"And he hit on me, too."

Marina rolled her eyes. "The point remains that we had the summer free. Louise doesn't have to be back at school until

September, and I'd quit my job at a discount mattress warehouse. We wanted to travel, do something with a goal, a cultural thrust. We made it our mission to hang out with people we admire. We wrote a fan letter, the literary form of the new century. We put our heads together, five glasses of wine into the night, and Louise typed the letter. About the St. Pierres, how 'Bushmills Threnody,' that entire album, is, like, wicked awesome."

"We wrote other people, too," Louise said shyly, "but your dad was the only one who wrote us back."

"Kurt Vonnegut never wrote back. Peter Bogdanovich neither."

"Well," Gord concluded, "it's good having you here." He pointed to the boombox on the table next to the Caesar salad, a sour, appraising look on his face, and looked at my dad: "What are we listening to?"

"The Rolling Stones. *Aftermath*. I just bought it on CD."

"Maybe that's the problem," Gord said, his face still and thoughtful. "CDs sound cleaner, but there's something missing."

"It's scientific fact that digital technology, the encoding process," Louise said, "is reductive. It takes nuance and texture in sound and turns them into ones and zeroes. It amounts to sonic fascism."

Gord nodded along. "These days," he said, "everything is political."

"Even the scratches, eh, Gord?" Nadine added, her mouth square and mocking.

"It's a warmer sound."

"Well, I guess I've missed the *sound*, since I've only listened to CDs. I've missed the *sound*," Nadine said. She rolled her eyes. Nadine always had to say something, be it about bad drivers or

How the Medication Makes Me Feel or the sound. "You people take everything that's old and crappy and call it an antique. Or retro. You give it another name, and something bad is good. It's so—so ridiculous. Some things are good and some things are icky."

"Can we eat peacefully this one night?" Dad said, his voice high and scolding, standing by the grill. He placed a hand to his chest and raised a tong to the sky, then lowered his voice. "Friends and neighbors, let us lay down our arms and sup."

"Ridiculous," Nadine felt compelled to add.

"Your dad baked a carrot cake," Marina said.

"I didn't know he baked."

"I did the corn and the potatoes. Louise tossed the salad," Marina continued. Then she whispered into my ear, giggling, "Louise likes your dad. Pass it on."

I watched them. Louise took occasional nips of Dad's beer, looking like a girl in fifth grade as she sat on her stool, her chest thrust forward, her feet resting on the stool's rung. I thought she was pretty stuck-up. It seemed as though she were waiting for someone to pronounce her the smartest and the prettiest, the only one who knew how to French inhale. She moved like a bird, her tiny head bobbing back and forth on her shoulders. She was fawning at my father. She kept touching Dad, his elbow, the small of his back. Dad smiled, his face newborn pink from alcohol as he sat down to eat. I almost remembered when I used to like him in spite of all his crap, when he could make an entire room quake with laughter.

The Caesar was a little oily, but I preferred oily to dry, and the corncob, prunish-looking but sweet. The meat was greasy and tangy, a little smoky.

"Louise," Marina said, "I thought you were a vegetarian."

Louise held a pork rib with her thumbs and forefingers, as one would a harmonica.

"I know, I know. I've fallen off the wagon."

We sat and ate quietly. The CD ended, and Dad set the stereo to the CBC, which was playing something West African. We watched Dad disappear into the house, Louise on his trail in a white sleeveless dress, her shoulders sagging.

Past the yard, past the fields beyond, cars coursed along the highway, their lights on in the twilight. The sky, from the horizon up, was orange, then pink, then a bloody, wet purple. The noise of traffic in the distance was soothing, the buzz of passing cars meshing with the bug zapper, which hummed by the screen door.

Nadine stood up, raised the boombox's volume, changing radio stations from the CBC to a top-forty station that was playing a Mariah Carey tune. While mouthing the lyrics, she took a seat on Gord's lap, twirling his thinning white hair in her fingers. They began whispering to one another and nuzzling. I liked Gord, but couldn't figure how he could suffer someone as mindless as Nadine. There were some things I didn't understand. My heart fell for a moment.

Marina smiled at me, her eyes heavy. She opened her mouth to say something but seemed to forget what was on her mind. Her mouth hung half open, her bottom lip wet. I decided then that my life would be a crushing defeat if I didn't at least stick my tongue down her throat in a private setting, somewhere dark. But I was just a young man, my hair goofy, my methods of seduction unproven, and my ludicrous father didn't make things any easier.

"How long has Dad been drinking today?" I asked Marina.

"Since the afternoon. He seems in pretty good shape, actually."

"Dad holds it pretty well until he starts throwing punches. What's the deal with him and Louise?"

"I went to bed early, so I can't say."

I mulled this over silently.

Then she added, almost purring, "You know, it was really her idea to come up here, more her idea than mine. I like the St. Pierres and all, but not as much as her. She was, like, wicked jealous about the French architect. She had a crush on the dis-gusting lech."

Dad and Louise emerged from the house reeking of weed, their faces red and guilty-looking. Louise's bra was showing as she carried out a half-eaten carrot cake in an aluminum dish.

"We sort of jumped the gun," Louise said.

Marina smiled, arching one eyebrow at me. At least he wasn't sleeping with the prettier one.

Dad held a big serving knife in one hand. He acted like the mother at a birthday party, a prissy, pretend schoolmarm, cut-ting little squares of carrot cake for us all. He took our plates and served the cake.

His eyes, bloodshot and blinking, landed on me.

"Saul," Dad said, "how was school?"

"Oh, you know. Business as usual."

A stupid smile spread over his face. Marijuana made him happy.

"I think you've turned into a fine young man, and I feel lucky that I didn't bugger that job."

"Thanks."

"Seventeen years old."

"Eighteen."

Dad turned to Gord, coughing into his armpit. "Take a look at him. Saul's eighteen, almost finished school."

Gord laughed. "Yeah, he's a big boy."

The radio station faded from the Mariah Carey tune to Urethra Franklin's "Bushmills Threnody."

Dad's eyes narrowed, his chin buried into his chest. He seemed upset for a moment, then he shrugged his shoulders and smiled. He pulled a lawn chair over to the picnic table and sat down.

"It's certainly catchy," he said. "I'll give them that."

"Urethra Franklin is like the Puff Daddy of Germany," Louise said. "This might well prove to be their crossover hit on this side of the Atlantic."

I sat picking at the crappy cake. The group's vocalist was rapping, his vocals megaphone-distorted and then electronically lowered in pitch.

"I can't really make out what he's singing," Louise said.

At this moment in history, this remade "Bushmills" belonged to a popular genre of music, wherein people sampled music, retooling and splicing it to fit their dance beats. Old songs were given new life. And if the members of Urethra Franklin were supposed to have a social conscience in this political world, it was all that much better. In their politicized worldview, my mother was cast as the voice of its ravaged indigenous populations.

"Is that English?" Nadine asked.

"Poverty ice cream," I suggested.

"Properly crimes," Marina said.

"Sounds like garbage to me," Gord grumbled.

"The song's supposed to be about native rights, unfair land treaties," Louise said. "Property is a crime."

"Whatever happened to melody? To good feelings? The energy here is way off."

"He's probably singing phonetically," Marina said.

The rapping stopped for a measure, and then my mother's voice kicked in with the chorus:

> I try to forget about you
> But you write, you telephone too
> Oh, my dear,
> Your hands so soft
> How can I sleep you off
> Like a hangover from the night before?

"I was thinking Tom Waits when I wrote this, early Tom Waits," Dad said. "Or the Moody Blues. It was supposed to feature a string section. Imagine a string section and an even slower tempo. Thankfully Leni sang the way she did—we had to change the song to suit her—and it sounds nothing like the Moody Blues."

"Did you know I was in an art rock band in college?" Louise said, turning to Marina. "We were called the Children of the Corn. I played kazoo."

"It wasn't supposed to be a single. The record company wanted the song as a b-side, but a disc jockey in Philadelphia, who had an advance copy, liked 'Bushmills' better. New singles had to be pressed soon afterwards."

"What was it?" Louise asked. "What was the a-side?"

"'Kelvin Technical Blues,'" Dad said.

All mothers weren't like mine. Jana said she had run off to be with an old lover. Helena St. Pierre hated touring, the whole rotten business. Jana was on the last St. Pierres tour. The first time she met my mother, the frail and thin native woman with Third World eyes, swollen and sunken, was backstage after a concert. Helena St. Pierre was sitting in a folding metal chair. It was strange, Jana thought, how everyone was ignoring her: the rhythm section eating cold cuts by the deli table next to her, the opening band griping about the sound check. My mother, dark and small. The truth was, she scared everyone on the tour. They were afraid to look her in the eyes, which at that moment were fixed on Jana.

"Am I in your chair?" she'd asked. Her voice was huskier than Jana thought it would be; she spoke slowly and tentatively. "Do you want it?"

Helena St. Pierre with a voice honey-tinged and full-bodied, lead-heavy.

Helena St. Pierre, a famous singer with a domineering husband and a big case of stage fright.

Helena St. Pierre, who hated being famous.

Helena St. Pierre, who became unhinged, who abandoned her husband and her newborn son to shack up with an old boyfriend.

While we spoke at my father's picnic table, the sky was turning the same weepy blue as the house. I could hear the crickets chirping against the radio's static. There was a sliver of silence as the song faded out, then the disc jockey named the last song, artist and title, before mentioning that only hours ago my mother had thrown herself out of an apartment window in Thailand.

Inside the house, the phone was ringing.

Every story retold carries a measure of vengeance. I lived in a world of voices, each one calling out for blood. I knew my mother only by hers. I heard Helena St. Pierre on the radio, making her comeback, voluntary or otherwise. When I heard my mother sing, I wondered what score she had to settle.

Tuesday

Jana drove me to school the next morning. Her car smelled like stale french fries, from too much drive-thru, our shared vice. Fries were jammed between the car seats and the hand brake, ketchup packets littering the ashtray. This was how a mother should smell—like fabric softener, like apple-scented conditioner and nail polish, like french fries.

She stopped the car at a school entrance. She ran a finger down my nose and *tsk*ed, then let me out behind a burgundy Volvo.

A clock by the cafeteria entrance read eight fifty-five. I turned left along the corridor leading to administration, running my knuckles against the lockers, feet squawking on the floor.

The school kept a trophy cabinet beside the office, a portrait of the queen and the prime minister. The secretary waved me through, as if truancy hung over me like a tarnished halo.

Our principal, Mr. Choi, leaned back in his chair, laughing on the phone. Another man stood beside him, resting a hand on top of a file cabinet.

Officer Dale pointed to a chair opposite Mr. Choi.

He stepped across the room, keys jangling on his belt, moving with a loud bounce, like a piano shoved over a speed bump. He went through his questions, scribbling down my information in his black vinyl notepad. Mr. Choi finished speaking on the phone. He looked sour and still, his hair heavily greased with patches of gray around his temples. I told Dale where I was yesterday.

Dale sucked in his gut and let it roll out.

"I didn't do anything," I said.

"That's all I wanted to hear, Saul. I honestly didn't think."

And so I stood up to go. The principal put down the phone as I reached the door.

"All done, are we?" he asked Dale. His face widened, the lines around his mouth creased disagreeably, bellowing like a hand organ. Mr. Choi was a weaselly autocrat who handed out suspensions to kids caught smoking. One girl found drunk at a school dance—the one who had "problems at home"—was expelled. "The boy has a history of troublemaking. He made a threat yesterday in his English class."

"What about it?" I sneered back. "I didn't do a fucking thing."

"Listen to him. Just listen."

Dale ignored him, nudging his head toward the hallway.

"I need to give a message to the boy's stepmother."

Dale followed me out into the hallway, waiting until a girl, an eleventh grader in a pair of bicycle shorts, passed us.

I slumped back against the lockers. I felt like heaving. That morning I'd had half a slice of dry toast and two extra-strength Tylenol for breakfast and chased it down with flat Pepsi from a two-liter bottle in the refrigerator.

"Son, I want you to know we can talk," Dale said. "That I take off this uniform when we speak."

I must have smirked.

"You know what I mean," he added.

"I'm all right."

He put his hand on my shoulder, his thumb brushing against my neck, and nodded solemnly. Dale smiled shyly, his face reddening. I wondered how Dale learned to be such a great communicator, whether he had taken classes on sympathy at police school, or if there were professional days devoted to the subject. We were both possessed with shame.

"Some crackpot phoned in this nerve gas business, complaining about a book that's being taught here, and the people here are looking for students to blame. That was just ridiculous, that interview," he said, hooking a finger in the loop of his belt. "Saul, you're a good kid, a real good piece of work—everything considered."

"Thanks."

"This may sound bad. He's still your father and you've got to give him that," he paused, "but I hear things about him from Jana. We were talking about you just yesterday."

"How was karaoke night?" I asked.

"It's on Wednesday," he said. "This is really crazy, this situation. Not karaoke night, but this toxic nerve gas situation. Because it didn't make anyone in this community look like hot poopoo. Everyone thinks we're backward here as it is because of the whole turban incident."

Dale had a hand on his belt, hiking it up and down. His face was red and he smiled crookedly, his eyes fixed on his nose.

"If I thought you were someone who was worth suspecting, I wouldn't be telling you, as I'm doing now, about the locker search at noon."

After my heart to heart with Dale, I ran into the washroom. At the sink I threw up, spewing out what looked like rancid spumoni. Then I wiped my face with brown paper towels that I had clumped into tragic little balls. I found a toilet stall with a lock on it. Snot skidded down my nose, and I coughed until my face was wet with tears.

I remained on my knees, elbows resting against the toilet bowl. There were two people there using the urinals. One of the fluorescent tubes buzzed on and off, making a rattling sound. The light here seemed to coat the entire washroom in a gray glaze. I didn't do anything; I didn't move.

I ran brown toilet paper along my eyes and threw up again.

Say you never knew your mother. Say she was some crazy native woman, a manic-depressive who went off, disappeared, when you were an infant. She left to be with another man. And your father shuts up whenever her name is mentioned. Say that everything you know about your parents you find in a paperback biography. Say that your mother's death leaves you a little confused. Because the only other dead people you knew were your grandparents, who died a week apart from one another when you were twelve. You miss them but can't exactly remember what they looked like, and now you think of them as you do the Magna Carta, like dates and names.

Say your mother was an absolute nutbar and she killed her-self because she hated hearing her voice on the radio.

Where was Thailand? Where the hell was it? Next to China, south of Korea, straddling the coast of whatever, drained by the river who cares, bounded by the hills of doesn't matter.

Underneath palm fronds and the tropical sun. She lived in Thailand, singing in a choir, teaching children to read, pleading with villagers not to sell their daughters. She lived by herself in an apartment complex near the church because only the priests and the nuns lived in the parish residence. Though she deemed herself too impure for the job, she kept her room the way she thought a novice's cell should appear: a single bed, the Bible on the nightstand next to an analog radio alarm clock, on the wall a picture of Christ shrink-wrapped in smoky plastic. She stayed on an almost liquid diet. Rice porridge and boiled cabbage. She was having back trouble. She placed a board under her mattress and slept on it. She mended her old dresses, polyester slacks twice torn, and secretly prayed to God that no one would recognize her there, as far east as she could get. She couldn't help thinking about her husband, her son, hoping they had forgotten her.

Where was Thailand?

Where my mother was.

No place at all.

The bell had just sounded. I stepped out into the hall, where students were already spilling out. A girl with red hair, a ninth grader, tapped my shoulder. She was wearing a spaghetti-strap top over a red bra. These days women were dressing sexier at a younger age. Hootchie. They showed skin and they jiggled

when they walked or line danced or shot putted. I couldn't
help myself around them.

She wanted my autograph.

"You're really him, right? I rollerbladed to your parents' song
last week."

I wrote my name in the lined notes section of her school
agenda, a little spiral-bound book with school holidays and
attendance rules listed in the front and, in the back, dated
pages to keep track of homework assignments.

"Whom should I make this out to?" I asked. And I thought
how silly that sounded coming from me. Whom should I make
this out to.

She took back her agenda, stared at the page and then
pressed it against her chest. She started away, but pivoted
around to face me.

"Hey, I just want to say, you know, sorry about your mom."

She hurried off, almost skipping, as if an invisible hand were
pushing her forward along the polished burgundy floors and
into second period.

This was how news traveled. Yesterday evening, right after we'd
heard about Helena St. Pierre's death, we moved inside silently,
our feet swishing through the backyard lawn, heels scuffing
against the bare kitchen floor as we entered the house. Dad had
slipped in first through the sliding-screen door to answer the
phone. Gord and Nadine went home. Marina foraged in the
refrigerator and found a bottle of vodka in the freezer and some
soda water, which had been at the back of the vegetable crisper.

Louise put a stack of dishes in the sink. Her wrists were
straw-thin, her cheeks rosy, her nose upturned. I could see how

Dad would go for her. It was her meek nature. She was like a waterlogged pastry, staring at me with her lips pursed, looking sort of frantic, as though she'd lost her passport or some other vital possession. Louise was about as small as my mother. Dad would like that. He hunched up his shoulders, he looked at you, his reading glasses sliding down his nose, like a scavenger. There was a lust for dead flesh stamped on his eyelids.

"You poor thing," she said.

I turned my back to her, glaring from the corners of my eyes. I began to follow Marina out of the room.

"Do you think it's a good idea for him to continue drinking?" Louise said, her voice a stage whisper. She opened the door underneath the sink and started scraping bones from plates into the trash with a fork. "I'm worried about him."

"Don't let it," I started to say, trailing off drunkenly.

"Don't let it what?" she asked.

"Don't let it keep you up at night."

In the living room, Marina sat on the couch, feet on the hassock. Her hands were folded on her lap, curled around a scotch tumbler. I dimmed the lights.

Marina's eyes closed as she yawned. "This is what I call a shit situation, Saul. A wicked shit situation."

"Don't look at me like that. Please."

She asked me what I meant.

"I hardly knew my mother, you know. It's no big deal."

She nodded. I sat down beside her on the black leather couch, which made a wheezing sound as I sunk into it.

"We can talk about normal things."

I sat there watching her.

Marina smiled, then bit her lip.

"Don't you have a girlfriend?"

"Um, not really."

My head fell against my chest. I stared meaningfully at my shoes, silently. I didn't have sufficient room in my heart for words. I was like my father, my miserable, sullen old man. Dad was a man of action, of cruel little gestures. He made me feel stupid not through put-down or criticism or even misplaced laughter, but by simply getting up for ice when I had anything to say.

I was like my father right now, sticking my hand up Marina's shirt.

Marina laughed as though she had been tickled. But her mouth stayed closed, and then she gently pried herself away from me.

I brought my face up to hers. I felt her breath on me. She had wonderful breath. I sat back.

"Sorry."

"Don't worry about it."

I could hear water running from the kitchen. Louise was doing the dishes. I was angry at her for being so stuck up, for adoring my father and fucking around with him now when he had more important things to deal with. I blurted out, "I hate her."

Marina took a sip from her tumbler, swallowing. "She's insecure."

"But she's so wonderful."

"She doesn't think anyone loves her."

"Well, tell her to get in line."

I took a little vodka from the bottle sitting on the coffee table. By then I was slurring from liquor, something that embarrassed me. I didn't hold alcohol well, and it seemed like I was at sea, rocking back and forth at half speed. I ran my hand across the back of my neck. I held my breath, wishing I could have five seconds back, thinking how desperate and sad I must sound to this woman who was older, sarcastic and slinky, sitting there with her mouth open, looking almost sinister, her bottom lip shiny and wet.

The lights rose back to full power and in came Dad, scratching his belly underneath his shirt.

He sat down next to us in the bentwood armchair, the chair creaking underneath his weight. He had been on the phone with my mother's lawyer in Bangkok. The lawyer had had trouble locating Dad's phone number among her belongings. His English wasn't very good, and Dad couldn't get much detail about what had happened. This is what I gathered.

"Has he been groping you?" Dad asked, off the topic, looking at me. He grunted. "Just like his old man. Has he asked you to the beach yet? Or to the waterslides?"

Marina laughed.

"The boy's cranked."

I made a gurgling sound, then I gave him the finger, wagging it in front of his face. It was something like an endearment from me to him.

"His grandfather, my old man, taught him that," Dad said. "The old man liked to curse. They thought he had that disease where you curse."

I could feel his breath against my ear.

"Well, it'll serve you right tomorrow. You little wet fart."

"I think he's asleep," Marina said.

He slapped his hand against my knee, a little harder than he needed to.

"Boy, do you want me to drive you home now?" he asked. "Or do you want to spend the night here?"

My eyes fluttered open, then closed.

All I could hear was my father's voice, speaking to his guests strong and keening and insistent, like a siren in traffic.

"Yeah," he said, "she'd been in Thailand for the last ten years, working as a missionary and singing in a church choir. First I heard of it. There was no note, says the priest. There was no sign of abnormal behavior. Normal. For Helena, that was always depending on how you looked at it. You were probably too young to remember it. A big scandal, in capital letters. It was in all the papers, on television and radio. Yeah. Labor Day, 1980. In town. Things were fine until then. Sure, we argued. Who doesn't argue? The rumor was that she heard the voice of God at a show. Yes, that God. Yes, that's what I gather. I can't say whether that's true. It happened very quickly. I can safely assume that she lost her gourd. She left the tour in the middle of a concert, left everyone in a blur, took a bus or a plane or a dog sled out of town. I held that bag, I did. Nearly bankrupted me. I still had to pay everyone, even if the tour was only half through. The insurance people said there was no clause for holy visions. No kidding. That was the last I heard of her. Didn't write, call. I didn't know she was in Thailand until just then. Last I heard she was in Toronto, living with some Chinese guy. Who knows what she'd been up to? I didn't care, but the boy—it was hard on the boy.

"But, no, don't feel as though you should leave. We've been getting along famously, and I think the boy likes you. You can tell. He's a shifty one, a dog, just like his wretched old man. Stay here as long as you want. I insist.

"They asked me what I wanted to do with the body. I told them to bring it over. Bastards. As if they were holding a cake for me. Like that. 'Should we ship it?' They gave me another phone number to call. Then I spoke to the kind priest. His name was Felix. He said he would handle it. Father Felix. Said Helena was a model missionary.

"I'll drive him home, I suppose. He's had a bad day. He deserves to wake up in his bed.

"The damned kitchen is a mess. Jana had wanted it done for years. She wanted a new house, practically. The woman thought I had gold hidden up my crack, she did. Well, I came into some money just recently and thought I should get it done. Just to prove that I get things done, but when I say they get done. It's going to cost ten thousand dollars.

"You put the salad bowl over there, in one of those cup-boards. You shouldn't bother. There. Ha, ha. You're a sweet-heart. Ha, ha. You're a gift."

Later that day, there was an announcement over the PA:

"Boys and girls, before third period begins, I'd like to say a few words. Yesterday, a very serious threat to your safety was made. I'm sure we all know by now what it was. It was a toxic nerve gas threat. And of course many students have been treating this whole thing as a joke—there are many 'humorous' people, it would seem."

For the rest of the afternoon, different blocks of students of Frances Brooke Secondary were called for inspection, beginning with those who had the strip of lockers along the hallway dividing the new gymnasium from the rest of the school. Our school was mostly brown kids, some white and fewer yellow. As far as I knew, I was the only native, even part-native, kid in school. We had specialty-foods days where we sampled samosas and pork buns. We casually approved miscegenation. That wasn't too bad. Actually, when a white kid and an Indian would date, it wasn't terribly scandalous, but it wasn't exactly commonplace. There were skinheads in the school, just like there were hippie and punk kids, but I don't think they were the racist kind of skinheads, just kids with shaved heads who liked the ambiguity. Besides, they were the ones who got picked on. It was the Sikh kids who rarely mixed—there was no great taboo, it just happened. They took most of the AP classes, the calculus and physics courses; they attended the peer-counseling sessions for university entrance. They sent away their transcripts for early admissions. They had hard-working, encouraging parents like Navi's, who wanted him to study law and spoke with half-British accents, like Navi's mother, who was a dentist, or not at all, like Navi's father, a pharmacist with exceptional, delicate manners. I quietly thought some of the Sikh kids obnoxious and loud, thumping basketballs on the cement courts that were also used for tennis, strolling down the hallways with their beat-boxes blaring their Indian dance music, bhangra or hip hop until an adult stepped out of a classroom and asked them to turn it off. These Sikhs were beefy guys in dark leather sports jackets and track pants. They tooled around in striped and finned Mustangs paid for from summers working at their fathers' construction companies laying cement for yet another box home. They had full beards at age twelve, swaths of hair between the joints of their fingers and their knuckles. They had bumper stickers declaring "Jat Power" or "Jats Do It Better!" A Jat, according to Navi, was an agrarian caste in India. I asked Navi whether he was a Jat. He shrugged his shoulders. He didn't hang out with other Sikh kids, just me. We hung out with each other and sometimes Rose. The running joke was that Navi and I belonged to the same tribe.

Students were to be at their lockers ready to open them; those who refused would have their locks cut off with bolt cutters. Officer Dale started at the beginning of the hall, flipping open locker doors with small mirrors and class schedules and pictures of Bollywood stars and singers taped to them, running his hands through suede jackets, rooting through textbooks, water-resistant Discmans and sour, wrinkly phys ed attire. There was garbage. There were sheaths of loose-leaf paper, empty lunch bags, drink boxes and darkened fruit rinds, which Officer Dale left on the floor as he made his way down the hall, getting less and less thorough.

"Having a good time, Officer Dale?"

Dale grunted. "I'm having a ball. A fucking ball."

I pointed to my locker, giving it a little kick. "It's in here."

Dale sighed. He must have figured, quite correctly, that we had all thrown away our toxic nerve gas fixings. At the open locker next to mine, he nodded absently, his fingers splayed across the side of his sanguine pouch of a face, his chin cupped by the heel of his hand, his elbow resting on his gut, his other arm folded across. He was sighing, looking bored, staring into a gray metal box as if it were speaking to him of desolation, of days like this. He glanced in my direction and shrugged.

"The nerve gas is in here. I've got it here."

I was tempting fate. Considering my luck, I should have had a big canister of cyanide, or whatever they use, in there, a fat gray keg of death, and people would gawk at me, mouths twisted, their expressions shocked and scornful. How could such a normal-looking boy, his father this, his mother ran, and then I would be arrested and locked up, where I could think long and hard about what I did. I winced when Dale opened the door. I bit my lip and scrunched my toes.

A note Rose wrote for me fluttered out, seesawing in the air.

After the locker search, I met up with Navi, and we left the school grounds. Navi was a little shorter than I, but just as bony, with a long, bulbous nose and lashy cow eyes. He was dabbling in fashion these days, having given up his T-shirts and high-tops for a more intellectual look—cardigans and tweed, hush puppies and a pair of horn-rimmed glasses that he bought without prescription at Safeway. He had clumsy, if fine and long, gray hands. In one of them, he held his trumpet, housed in a leather case with snap locks and a black plastic handle.

We got lunch at the twenty-four-hour convenience store and gas station across the street. There I deliberated over a selection of iced teas, settling on Lipton, while Navi heated vegetarian Jamaican patties in the microwave by the coffee and espresso makers. By that time, I figured I was on an upswing: my head still hurt, but my stomach had settled down. Next to the counter was the local morning tabloid. On its cover was a photo of Helena St. Pierre at an airport, one of those archival shots that implied misfortune by how dated, how seriously outside fashion, the people photographed were. Here in this picture, she wore a pale cream trenchcoat, her belt cinched tight to give her an ass, and

Porsche wraparound sunglasses. Her hair was parted in the middle, dropping down to her waist. Her face seemed narrow. She was alone, one of the few photos without my father. Though not really—there he was, in the bottom left-hand corner of the photograph, a hand on my mother's elbow, leading her away.

I waited outside, quaffing iced tea, as Navi paid for his patties. Then we stood under the store's orange sign, next to an orange trash bin, facing empty parking slots and midday traffic.

Anders Wong, our town's only homeless man, was carrying empty pop cans in a Safeway cart.

"Follow me. Let me take you somewhere," he said. "By a ditch is a burlap sack filled with pornography."

"How did you find it?" Navi asked.

"It's my sack." He dug out a Mountain Dew can in a trash bin and dropped it in his cart. "The authorities harbor serious hubba-hubba for beaver shots. They'd take it if they found it. It's my prize possession, my oeuvre—but I offer it to you."

"Why?"

"Look at me," Anders said. He dropped his cans and brought his face close to us, pointing at himself with his grimy right index finger. His eyes were narrow and rimmed with sleep. He had a fine, girlish mouth offset by eyebrows that almost came together. There was something stuck to his chin—orange peel. "Look at this face. Can't you see?"

Navi and I looked, stroking our chins until Anders finally gave up on our guessing and blurted out, "I'm in love."

"What's it like?" I asked bashfully.

Anders looked to the ground. He paced around in a circle, his face shriveling in spite.

"My baby's left me for another man. My baby's heart is a lump of coal."

We went to the hardware store at the strip mall down the street. I asked a man in a tie and a blue vest where they kept the spray paint. He gave me a snotty look, eyebrows raised, before leading us down an aisle to the far end of the store. The spray paints were arranged by color, black to yellow, on a rack. I found some gold sparkle and rattled the can in my hand, then started forming imaginary letters in the air, as if I were practising tai chi, like Rose's parents.

"I don't want to butt in or anything," the man in the vest said, "but you'll be going to court and they'll make you work off the damages. They have records. It'll be damn near impossible to cross the border."

I nodded toward Navi.

"We're painting his sister's bike. Do you have this with more sparkle?"

The guy in the vest shook his head. "Tell it to the judge, boys."

We stood at an intersection, watching elementary school kids crossing. There was a woman across the street at the store. I thought it was Marina, and my heart skipped.

Navi once-overed me, his watery eyes gliding over my face. He gulped and gasped. Then his eyes shut as if he were about to sneeze.

"The locker check was heinous," Navi said. "I'm passing around a petition at three o'clock in protest."

I nodded. He handed me a copy. There were seventy-eight signatures on it already—quite a few of them with the same handwriting. Navi doubted the efficacy of petitions, of conventional methods of change, but he nevertheless felt the system had to be engaged, that it would crumble under close scrutiny. I believed this, too, maybe with less ardor, but enough to play along.

Navi began crying.

"Your mother killed herself," Navi said, getting to the heart of the matter.

"That's what they say."

Navi ran the cuff of his sports jacket along his eyes.

"It's okay," I said to him, patting his shoulder. He pulled me into an embrace, and I fell against him, uneasily at first. I envied Navi, how freely his feelings came to him, and how they sort of fell out of him, perfectly formed.

Then I heard someone call my name. It was Marina at the gas station parking lot.

Anders was talking to her.

"My baby's left me," he said. "She left me for another man. Gone. She made me harder than Cyrillic algebra."

"Maybe I've got the exchange rate wrong or something, but I still don't get it. I mean why are cigarettes," Marina said, "like, thirty-seven dollars in this country?"

"To pay for health care," I said.

"To kill off the rich," Navi said.

Marina was in a jean jacket with a Skid Row band logo drawn on the back in blue felt-tip. She smiled at me quickly, and the blood rose to my face and my neck.

"I've been sitting around all day," she said, "then I walked into your beautiful town, helped an old man carry groceries to his car, bought cigarettes. Reporters have been ringing all morning.

There have been crank calls. Meanwhile Louise is in the study revising her screenplay's first plot point—like she hasn't done that a million times already. Your dad's been taking phone calls, arranging for the funeral. Ian said the body will be here by Saturday night. That's how long it's going to take to clear customs."

"That long?"

"By then," she said, "the German documentary film crew will have arrived. There's a major TV special in the making."

I nodded, trying to hide my bewilderment.

"I can hardly wait," I said.

But here I was, waiting. Not by choice. We were all sitting around waiting for the world to come to us.

Dinner was the only time someone wasn't playing music in the Samra house, with its creamy plush carpeting and pink wallpaper. Their home was strewn with sheet music, music stands, instrument cases, and banged-up brass and string instruments. Navi was, like me, cursed with a musical family.

The family, including aunts, uncles and grandparents, ate smorgasbord-style every night—stewed lentils and vegetables in deep aluminum dishes—with paper plates and a patterned vinyl tablecloth over the dining-room table. There wasn't a table that could seat the entire family, so we spread out in different rooms around the house, balancing our food on our laps. I sat on a scratchy, yellow linen couch in the family room between Navi and his twelve-year-old sister, Priti, while Marvin and Kavie lay in front of the television playing video games. Edmond looked on, anxious to play.

I'd envied Navi's family since my first sleepover here in sixth grade, in spite of the crowding and the bickering that came with such numbers. I watched Edmond start crying and Navi roll his eyes—his little brother always did this when he couldn't get his way. I still envied him.

An old woman—Navi's grandmother, I think, visiting from India—sat in a folding chair talking on a wireless phone. She told Marvin to let Edmond have his turn at the Sony Playstation. Marvin was an ugly kid with a droopy nose and a bowl cut—it was tragic. He was the only person allowed to play the Steinway, which he had won at a national competition in Ottawa. Priti, who was tall and wore square, plastic-rimmed glasses, asked me about electives for when she entered high school in September. I urged her to register for Miss Adler's drawing class. Priti's twin sister, Jaya, away that night at a jazz choir rehearsal, was weird and obsessed with uniforms. She was begging her parents to send her to Catholic school. I thought Jaya was prettier, but Priti had a nicer smile. Sandeep, who was wearing a long, tangly Van Dyke with a lentil stuck to it, walked into the room looking for his wah-wah pedal. Marvin told him that it was upstairs in his room, the one he shared with Edmond and Kavie.

Navi was in a hurry to finish. As we were about to leave, Navi's mom asked us what we were up to.

"We're going to school," Navi said, standing at the door. The cans of spray paint clinked in my bag. "We're rehearsing a play. *Rhinoceros.*"

"Ionesco," she said. She kissed Navi on the forehead, which made me feel a little sad. "Then have a good practice."

We sat on the bleachers in front of the soccer field, waiting for it to get dark. We sat there flipping through the pictures Navi took yesterday. They were of confused crowds and men in masks, blurry and underlit. Navi owned a Polaroid and a Nikon he signed out from the photography club and never returned. He was the official yearbook photographer, or so he told everyone, but I seriously doubted his ability to pull one over on the editorial staff. We all had serious doubts. He was a compulsive picture taker, even if, in his case, ability staggered behind enthusiasm. He had pictures of outstretched hands and frowns and underwear waistbands. There were other photos from the same roll. Pictures of people chewing, shot from behind. Photos of me sleeping, where I look absolutely blissful, like a newborn corpse.

By now it was almost dark. I had to be at Rose's in fifteen minutes.

We weren't very good at topical slogans: on the staff parking lot, we painted "Live Nude Girls" in hot-pink lettering, then "Police State Secondary," and then on the wall beside the main entrance, we wrote "Shithead." We stood at the edge of the parking lot, inspecting our work.

"Well, what do you think?"

Navi nodded. We tried to keep our expectations low.

"What do you think?" he asked.

In response to censorship, I suggested we should plan a walkout. Navi liked the idea. In response to book bannings and anonymous threats and the state of the world, we should all just pack up and leave.

In the distance, we heard some muffled crying, then saw Anders emerge from the Dumpster, still sobbing about his baby.

That afternoon Rose had left this note in my locker:

> Hi! Western Civ never ceases to bore me. Mr. Plant is having the class form small groups in order for us to make presentations on various systems of government on Thursday. I think he's—as you would say—"on crack" and doesn't want to teach. I'm sorry I yelled at you yesterday. [Here she drew a frowning face.] I was having a bad day. For second period, we're going on a trip to the planetarium. I feel a little old for the planetarium, but still think it will be fun!!! I won't see you today, but I need to talk to you. It's important!!! Tried calling you last night, but you weren't home. xoxo

Rose lived in a new development, where the houses had three-car garages, with Lexuses and Range Rovers parked outside. There were wide front yards cluttered with shrubbery and pine saplings attached to wooden stakes, but few gardens, sometimes only arrangements of rocks where flowers should have been. She had a separate entrance to her suite. Her parents had it built when her aunt lived with them—until she married a geologist and moved to the Yukon. When Rose answered her door that night, she was in sweats, her hair tied in pigtails. The light outside clicked on. There was a motion detector that lit up whenever anything moved in the backyard.

"You're late," she said. "Take off your boots."

I sat on her bed and yanked off my boots. I put my jacket, an English-style rain jacket, at the foot of her narrow bed, moving aside a geography textbook and placing it on her nightstand atop her radio alarm clock, with the lime green LED display.

Rose stood in front of me, leaning against my knee. I placed my cold hands up her sweatshirt and ran them along her soft belly, feeling her quiver. Rose smiled, then backed away and disappeared into her bathroom.

I heard the tap run, then the motion of her toothbrush. It was a wonderful sound, the sound of her spearmint breath. This was what I liked most about her house, about her—not only the cleanliness, but the effort, the energy put into removing the grimy and unsavory.

The bathroom door slid open, and she came out flossing her teeth.

She sat next to me on the bed, and I put my arm around her waist. She gave off a scrubbed, pink heat.

I fell on top of her.

She didn't ask any questions about Helena St. Pierre. She knew me well enough not to, and I appreciated that. I lifted the sweatshirt over her head and let her undo her bra. We lay down on the very narrow bed, my back almost pressed against the wall as we tangled limbs, her short fingernails grazing down my chest.

"I'm getting fat again."

"I haven't noticed."

She had been sick for two months, at home much of that time, alone or with her dad, who took a leave of absence to feed her cream of mushroom soup and watch movies with her as the afternoon sun crossed over their living-room skylight. And when she had come back to school, her body, which had been almost boxy, finally matched her mother's quarter-Gypsy face—her dark hair, her soft, doughy cheeks and eyebrows that arched over her forehead like the legs of a spider.

Rose's head was pressed against her neck so that she had a double chin. And there was a film coating her eyes that seemed childish, but immeasurably beguiling, if only because I knew how to make it disappear, to make her feel good.

"How do you like being kissed?" I asked her.

"I don't know. I just like being kissed."

"Like this?"

"That's nice."

"Thank you."

She rubbed her knee against my crotch and placed her head against my chest.

"What are you thinking?" she asked me.

The lights clicked on outside. Sometimes cats or raccoons would run through the yard and the light would seep through her curtains.

I was thinking of my beautiful mother, but lied and said I didn't know.

"What do you mean you don't know?"

"I don't really think hard about what I'm thinking," I said.

I was thinking about my shit luck. I was my father's son. I was the son of a cheap, embittered lecher.

"What do you mean by that?" she asked.

"I don't know. I just said it."

"Why don't you ever ask me what I'm thinking?"

"I respect other people's mysteries."

"If I died, would you miss me?"

I nodded.

"Would you be really upset?"

I nodded again.

Somebody knocked at the door, the one to Rose's suite.

"It's my mom," she said. "She probably heard us talking."

"Don't answer."

"She's knocking."

"If you don't answer, she'll think you're asleep."

"It's only nine-thirty. She'll just keep knocking."

"Be quiet."

"Okay."

"Quiet."

I could only picture her cast in smog, half lit, surrounded by a huddle of men, blocked by someone's head. The priest my father spoke to said she worked with young women. Long ago in the sixties—almost two lives ago—she'd learned to make dresses from her grandmother and picked up beauty tips and poise from work. She'd been at a cosmetics counter selling makeup at the Bay. That was her last job. She'd been trained in women's work. Now she did light secretarial tasks, taught some English, gave sewing classes.

She always liked to watch cartoons. During the summer, in the unbroken humidity, they would sit outside under the palm trees, in the field next to the door. The girls waved fans and drank from cans of cherry soda. They watched cartoons dubbed into Thai on a television wheeled outside from the Sunday school. She and the nuns hung back on hard classroom chairs. The nuns would go to bed first. She would stay outside as long as the cartoons played, until she fell asleep. These days when she slept, it was difficult to wake her. Sometimes, the girls would have to shake her.

One night, she found herself being tickled. Two of the younger girls were running their hands along her ribs. She twisted, half awake, and fell on the ground, her mouth open like

a cracked oyster. The two girls shrieked in laughter. Leni's eyes
followed them until they ran back into the dorm, hand in hand.

According to reports, Helena St. Pierre died shortly after an
encounter with a television crew.

Once, out of curiosity, she managed to get into a sex club—it
was a slow night. She paid the teenage bouncer with the faint
mustachio a few extra baht and was let into a room where she
saw them in the adjoining room, almost pageant-like, in identi-
cal gowns. Yellow gowns with numbered badges. When she
worked at the Bay in the sixties, they'd given her a uniform with
a badge on it, and occasionally she'd modeled swimwear—it had
all seemed so innocent back then.

There were two tourists in the room with her—an Asian and
a European. The European pulled out a disposable camera,
aimed and snapped. The announcer in the room eagle-clawed
his mike, whispered over his shoulder, and the photographer was
out on his rear, pushed through the bar, face down on the street.

It had never been easy for her. It was in her best interests to
hear her voice at the dry cleaners.

A reporter arrived at her door, seeking an interview. This came
four days after hearing her voice playing in a bar, two days after
the priest approached her with a magazine and a pen. She heard
her tune hummed by one of her girls, and stared at her cockeyed.

They—*they*—wanted humiliation memorialized. Their
video tape slathered the air around them, around you, in
formaldehyde. They were like ancient pharaohs: killing you as
though to place you in their own graves, for you to serve them
in the netherworld. Fearing death, they killed you.

Wednesday

Marina put Louise in a headlock. She kissed the side of her head, just above her temple. Louise curled up on the couch, dropping her head in Marina's lap. Her eyes were wet. Louise began laughing, then Marina. They squealed until they were gasping, their eyes merry. Marina carried her long, steep nose with aplomb, her blondeness, bangs cut straight across her head, set against her pale gray eyes. Louise was thin and had a face the shape of a pumpkin seed, her chin pointing out abruptly. Her mouth was too small for her tiny face.

I had decided to cut class for the day and went to my father's home. I couldn't think straight, I couldn't sleep, and I figured this was the place to be.

"There was an argument last night," Marina said.

Trust Dad to pick a fight, I thought. Trust him to cause trouble.

"We were sitting around," Louise said. "Ian was reading his hate mail. He said I was looking at him funny. I asked him what he meant. 'Oh, nothing. You're just looking at me funny.'"

Louise started to cry again.

"I mean, who wouldn't want to be told they were loved?" Marina asked. "Even if they didn't feel the same way."

Louise disentangled herself from Marina and stood up. She flipped through a magazine on her lap with one hand, chewing the thumbnail of the other.

"I think he wants to sleep with you," she said.

"Do you think?"

Louise glared at Marina.

"Don't get so excited," she said. A shadow fell across her face. "I only said he might because I wanted to see how you would react."

"How'd I do?"

Louise snorted.

I looked out the window, my stomach growling. It was alarmingly bright outside. The sun had begun hitching its way up the sky, which was a bleached, blurry white, daylight ringing off windshields of cars trickling along the highway, giving the furry evergreen in the yard a stout, overdressed appearance. Dad was outside speaking to a man with spiky, hennaed hair. Spiky-hair guy wore a pressed white shirt—the top three buttons were undone, exposing pinkish skin.

"That's Richard. He arrived early this morning to produce a segment for a German television network."

Richard was gesturing royally, his hands above his head, waving them like he was a television weatherman in front of an imaginary weather map. Dad looked serious, his gut flung out, scratching his head thoughtfully. He was pointing to the distance, to cow pastures with run-down fencing, past a bill-board beside the highway advertising car rentals.

"The old man likes being on TV," I said.

"Yeah, we figured," Marina said.

Louise started running the heel of her palm over her eyes, almond shaped, almost Asian. She was in a cheery red polka-dot blouse, the sleeves unbuttoned and slipping from her elbows. She rubbed the back of her neck and frowned.

Louise stood up and began rolling her neck along her shoulders. She raised her hands up, palms out, toward the ceiling and yawned. She bent down and stood on her hands, exposing a flat white belly and baby-blue ankle socks. Louise, her feet in the air, gave a wobbly smile.

"What are you doing?" Marina asked.

"Giving a damn."

The coffeemaker sat on the counter beside a piece of orange tarp and the old, gutted kitchen sink. Dad wanted to know whether I wanted anything. He offered me coffee, which I declined, then took his with cream. Richard and Dad's visitors were going to Pappalardi's, a local diner. Dad said he didn't want breakfast, there was business that needed looking after, but that I should go before heading off to school.

"Do you think I should be in Thailand?"

I shrugged my shoulders. I was taller than he was, thinner. I stared at his bare feet and saw gray hair on his toes.

"Look at me when I talk to you," he said. "I feel like you're trying to sell me a car."

"Sure."

"Do you know how much a fucking flight to Thailand costs?"

"I don't know, Dad." I looked around the demolished kitchen. "Ten thousand dollars?"

"That's very funny."

"Hey, no one's asking you to go."

"I'm just worried about you. I don't want this whole business to be too much bother," Dad said. "School's important. Look at me. I didn't go to school. You can see what a sorry wreck I am."

My mind drifted during Dad's stab at self-deprecation. There were tools on the kitchen counter left there by Gord. I picked up a tape measure and started yanking it out a foot, then letting it slide back into the metal casing. Dad snapped the measure away from me and put it back on the counter.

"Would you please not play with all this crap. It's bad enough that Gord stopped working on it yesterday."

"Is he sick?"

"Nadine's been hospitalized. I tell the woman the hamburger was fully cooked, but she insists otherwise. 'Well, have it your way,' I say to her."

"Have you heard anything from the lawyers?" I asked.

"Your mother wasn't rich. Don't worry about that. We were surprised she had any money at all. Not a lot, less after taxes and legal costs, but what little she had she'd decided to give to the Church. You'd think the woman would've taken better care of herself. She was living in a sty."

Dad took a sip of his coffee, then chuckled into his favorite mug, the one with the Edward Hopper diner scene reproduced on its surface.

"That sounds funny," Dad said. "Didn't that sound funny?"

"What?"

"When I called Helena your mother."

"What?"

"Forget about it."

"Get to the point."

"You cutting classes, hanging around here. You didn't even know the woman."

"She was my mother."

"Jana's your mother. I mean, I don't know why you're so upset. Or is this your way of getting attention."

Dad set his coffee mug at the edge of the counter, beside the sink filled with dishes that Louise had yet to attend to, and turned away. I swatted the mug to the ground with an open fist. It broke into three pieces.

"What do you want from me? What do you expect from me?" My voice rose high and nasal like his.

Dad turned back, his face red and startled.

"For Christ's sake, Saulie—if you're going to sulk."

"Dad, help me out here."

"I'll help you. Sure, that's what I'm here for. I'm everyone's fucking wet nurse."

"If she's not my mother, who is she?"

"What is wrong with you?" Dad said. It was as though I blinked just to catch his spit in my eye. "Oh, Christ. Please don't cry."

"I'm not crying."

"Yeah, whatever."

He knitted his brow and his chest heaved. He bent down to the floor, picking up two pieces of the mug, pressing them together to see whether it could be fixed with glue. The handle piece still lay on the ground. I lifted my foot and kicked it with my toe across the room. It skidded along the linoleum, then stopped by the kitchen table with the chairs stacked on top of it.

"What is this?" Dad said. I lunged at him like a grade-school bully, and then fell back at the last moment. I saw my cowardly father wince, an open hand raised in front of his face.

"Who the hell was she?" I asked.

"Who?"

"My mother."

"Not who you think she was." Dad mumbled something under his breath. "We're having a funeral for her. I figured it would be more dignified than leaving her out on the curb."

Richard bought us omelets and hotcakes at Pappalardi's, a family restaurant popular with old people in sun hats and white belts, and servers scooting around in their mushroom-gravy brown uniforms, serving French toast or returning with extra cream. I ate quickly, finishing my order of hotcakes before my orange juice arrived, smothering my bacon with maple syrup from a dispenser that got my fingers all sticky. Richard sat stewing, unable to smoke his hand-rolled cigarettes inside, worried that his cameraman, Andreas, whom he was to meet that afternoon, had missed a connection in Boston.

"So, how long have you been a reporter?" Louise asked.

Richard looked at Louise, not exactly glaring, his forehead wrinkling in irritation. It took him a moment to collect himself, his face softening again, before he could answer.

"I am not a reporter, even if my background might suggest journalist. There is not exactly a word for it in your language. My position at the network roughly translates as 'cultural critic.'"

"We have cultural critics here, too," Marina said. A waitress was removing our dishes. Richard once-overed her, then looked away.

"My English is poor," Richard said. "I am more like a cultural *interrogator*."

"That's what they're called," Louise offered. "Cultural critics."

"They told me I was too good-looking to be taken seriously," Richard said.

"You proved them wrong," Louise said.

"I hosted a prize show in which contestants won money for medical treatments. The contestants had serious ailments—cancer or AIDS, whatever. They were asked to climb the third highest mountain in the country. Or to pull a car with their teeth. They—the network—said test audiences found my melancholy preposterous."

"Wrong again."

Richard ran the heel of his hand along the back of his neck, his mouth set sternly. "Yeah, their assumptions proved false. This is true." He said this matter-of-factly, his *g*s hard and vowels swift. He was a pretty man, his cheekbones prominent and teeth gapped. He moved his hands effeminately as he filled out his credit-card receipt. I listened to Richard talk about Helena St. Pierre—uncovering and handling her life had become his obsession, he said—and I wondered what my own claim on her was. Maybe my father was right—I was acting out for sympathy. But I heard her name spoken and felt a twinge.

"She was born left-handed, but taught by priests to write with her other hand," Richard was saying. "Her childhood pet was an Irish setter named Toby. She had bad teeth, which had to be capped twice. She fell off a bike as a child and had a

discolored front tooth, like Indian corn—ha, ha. Her first sex-
ual experience was at age twelve, with a boy at school named
Leonard who offered her grape soda. She was an exhibitionist,
she called polyester slacks patriarchal. She never had a driver's
license. Her favorite color was white. She only ate foods that
were white—toast and butter and skim milk—when she was
hospitalized. She collected postcards when she first started
touring. Later, tours and concerts would be delayed because
she would be hiding. In closets, in movie theaters. She arrived
in Thailand in 1982. Her grandmother's dying wish—she died
in 1991—was that she return to her family. She was an artist;
she made people cut her food for her."

The waitress took the bill. We left the restaurant and
headed to Richard's car. Marina wanted to know whether I
wanted to join them in the city this afternoon. Part of
Richard's assignment in Western Canada involved coverage
of Urethra Franklin's tour, which had included shows in
Toronto and Montreal this past weekend, and a concert in
town Saturday.

"The Franklins are at the CD superstore in the city," Marina
said, "holding a press conference and autograph session after a
short acoustic set."

"Aren't they an electronic band?" I asked.

"I think they'll be blowing seashells or something."

Richard's rental car was parked at the end of the drag, in the
lot of the IGA. Much pride was taken in our renewed downtown core. There was the main drag with its brick and lime-
stone facades, the fire hydrants newly painted red with white
trim, the Home Hardware outlet and the tiny elm trees fenced
in black wrought iron. Banners hung from the streetlights:

"Renewing our Past!" and "Free Weekend Parking!" and "Visit the Harbor Front Mall!" A fire station had been converted into the new heritage museum, a place where one could learn about the native population that inhabited the area in the first part of the nineteenth century and an early Chinese settlement, former railroad laborers and destitute prospectors, whose plywood shacks burned down in the 1890s after a stove exploded. The only building to survive that fire was the brothel, which had become the museum. Across the street from the heritage museum was Pappalardi's.

The car was in sight when we turned to see Louise in front of a used bookstore. She was squatting underneath the awning, scratching her finger at the window. She was cooing at a marmalade-colored house cat balled up in a wicker basket inside the display window. It stood, arching its back, and raced along the display in front of a hardcover edition of *The St. Pierres' Story* by Leslie Erickson. The dust jacket featured a picture of my parents, faded with coffee stains splashed across it in crescent half-moons. This was what happened when you achieved notoriety: you gained objecthood, you became a coaster. On the cover photo was my mother, her chin obscured by a microphone, holding a tambourine at her hip, my father, wearing a turtleneck, shadowy behind the spotlight, strumming a twelve-string sullenly. The very same cover picture could be found on the paperback edition I owned, plus in a fifteen-page insert of color photos, squirreled away with a pile of photographs of my mother and an old pair of jeans that belonged to her.

"You don't mind," Louise asked, "if I take a look inside?"

Richard wanted to call his cameraman; Marina stayed

underneath the green awning to finish a cigarette. Louise pushed the door open and crossed an infrared tripwire, which announced her presence with two electronic bell chimes. The cat jumped out from the front window and disappeared behind the front counter.

I followed her in. The store was narrow, like all the other shops on this strip, and smelled of sandalwood. The bookstore owner was an Asian man in his forties wearing a Killdozer T-shirt and a shaggy gray beard. His eyes followed Louise as she went through paperback romances and spy thrillers in the bargain bin.

I took the copy of the St. Pierres biography from the display window and flipped through it. In perfect honesty, maybe the only book I had read all the way through might have been my parents' biography, which I picked up every month or so, slogging through the boring trivia about their first record contract. Or the critical analyses of their first album, A *Home on Blind River*, and the second one, *Prairie Winds*, which was recorded on honey slides—hash panfried with honey—versus their more electric third album, the megahit *Bushmills Threnody*, in 1973. There was commentary about CRTC legislation that set quotas of Canadian music on commercial radio stations, and how it altered Canadian folk music the same way Bob Dylan did in America when he plugged in a Fender Telecaster at the 1966 Newport Folk Festival. I handled the book gingerly.

Say you never knew your mother and say when she killed herself you felt bad in some ways, but maybe you didn't feel bad enough. Because you were not sure whether you hated her as your father did. And say she was gorgeous.

Say your mother was a model, a conceptual artist, a teenager who had moved to Toronto in 1969. She was already making a name for herself through her public displays of nudity, posing on street corners, in front of a department store in the name of peace. She was like that—starving, mouth gaping for attention, for what she would eventually throw away.

Your father had also recently arrived from Winnipeg, via Fort William, where he had been doing Beatles and Kinks covers at a place called the Red Eye, traveling out here in a retired ambulance. His weekends were spent on Yonge Street, in taverns called Le Coq d'Or and the Colonial, gigging with an R&B group called the Resistors because everyone else in the band was a draft dodger. His grandfather had died and left a small legacy, enough to buy a twelve-string Guild. He would write his songs in bed, drinking jasmine tea, spitting tea leaves onto the floor of his room, which gathered next to dustballs and paperbacks. During the week, he would skulk around Yorkville to watch the folkies perform in ill-lit cafes and communes. Near Gerrard was the Bohemian Embassy, where singers served as comic relief between poetry readings, and on Avenue Road was the New Gates of Cleve, where you might find Joni Mitchell, fresh out of art school in the Prairies, or the Tysons singing "Four Strong Winds" or something new that Gordon Lightfoot had just written, or Neil Young at Club Bluenote with the Mynah Birds (named after another coffeehouse with a nude chef), his band with Rick James here from Buffalo to avoid naval duty.

And one evening your father is onstage at an unlicensed basement venue, singing a number he wrote about his sister who died of polio—another great pain that goes undisclosed—when he catches your mother flicking past the beaded entrance, floating behind a tasseled lamp, talking to some panty-waist, who everyone here knows is a painter or a writer or something. And your father thinks he can rub out Van Gogh with his fretting hand tied behind his back.

His voice cracks. He sings too softly, your father the drunk, the gutter mouth, with a straight face:

> I want to know what secret takes hold
> When she turns away
> I want to know what weighs on her soul
> When she doesn't say
>
> What hurt she must know, a doubling hole
> Grows inside her heart
> What hurt in her wakes, inside her aches
> What is torn apart?
>
> Shining brightly, shining lightly
> Her eyes warm my eyes
>
> For if I had it, the secret to her sadness
> I would hide it far away
> To the stars above, I would fill her heart with love
> now and everyday
>
> Shining brightly, shining lightly
> Her eyes warm the night
> Shimmering lovely, glimmering lovely
> Her eyes warm my eyes

Your mother, fresh off a bad relationship, eats it up.

"Are you much of a reader?" Louise asked.

"Not really," I said.

Louise smirked. She reached into her pocket and found an elastic, then pulled her hair back. I watched her rub the back of her neck, her fingers running over a hickey, and head toward the rear of the store. The dark ponytail bobbed like a shiny fishing lure. I followed her.

We were facing a narrow shelf of books. At the top, written in red ink on a lined index card, was "Canadian Literature."

"I can't say I read too much, either," Louise said, putting down a copy of *Owls in the Family*.

"But you're a writer."

"Screenwriter. Letter-writer."

"Same shit, different piles."

"That's the problem with the world."

"What is?" I asked.

"Too many writers, not enough readers."

Louise bent down, running her finger past all the spines.

"That's the problem with your father," she said. "There aren't enough people willing to listen to his story. They would sooner make up their own. That's why your father wants to talk."

"Of course he does."

"If he were so terrible, like everyone says, people wouldn't care about him. Your mother, your stepmother."

"Should I call you Mom?"

"I think Marina has her eye on him."

I absolutely loathed her.

"Forget about it, all right," she said. "Pretend this conversation never happened. At least you're keeping her occupied— for now. That I'm glad about."

"What does that mean?"

"It means," she said, plucking a paperback from the shelf, "that I've found my book, so now we can leave."

At the counter, the guy in the Killdozer shirt rang up Louise's purchase, *hmm*ing approval of her selection.

Marina and Richard were waiting for us outside.

"Can you drive me home, back to Ian's?" Louise asked.

"What did you buy?" Marina asked.

Louise held up the book. The title was familiar: *Baroque-a-Nova.*

"This nerve gas threat someone called in," I said, "was over that."

"Never read it," Marina said.

"I've been meaning to read it," Louise said. "It's Cancon."

"What?"

"Canadian content," Louise said.

She shook her head at Marina, the American, who stuck her tongue out at Louise and huffed, "Don't be like that. Just because I can't tell you what the capital of Moose Jaw is. I'm not expected to know everything."

Richard drove only Japanese cars. For that reason I was in the driver's seat of his maroon Ford Tempo when Marina pointed out the sign to me. We had turned at the town's main intersection and were passing the high, green fencing that blocked off the highway from the housing developments. I turned back to see.

Seagulls were circling in the sky above. The message was written on a bed sheet in pink lettering: "Helena St. Pierre: 1950–1998." Since my own father thought I was making a big deal of the whole situation, I didn't know why anyone else would give a damn. Maybe there were people here who were moved by her voice. They saw her play live and went home with her voice in their heads. Maybe they owned her albums, clipped out her photos. Maybe they straightened their hair to look like her. Or they paid money to join the official St. Pierres Appreciation Society, located in Thurso, Scotland. Or maybe it was their parents who raised them on Helena St. Pierre, maybe they grew up with her. Imagine that. I looked at that crude sign with more wonder than it probably deserved, as though it were directed at me. An invitation. I didn't know under which terms I could accept it.

Richard pointed to the Silver and Gold Motor Inn, where he was staying. It was obscured by tall spruces, but one could still make out the domed structure, painted lime green, long faded, that housed its tennis courts, and beside that, a billboard flashing the time and temperature.

"Wednesday is karaoke night," he said.

"Ooh, karaoke night," Marina said.

Richard's spirits had picked up after learning his cameraman was on a standby flight and would arrive in time for the press conference. He looked sunny in the passenger-side front seat, wearing his designer sunglasses, holding a bottle of iced cappuccino.

"I look forward to interviewing Saul for my show."

"That's if he's interested," Marina said. She caught my eye in the rearview window, and I looked at her as if she was joking.

"He seems like the interview-shy type. He keeps his cards against his chest. That's why I like him."

"People show much fascination in the children," he said, sounding defensive. When he brooded it looked as though he were chewing the inside of his mouth. "Of course, all children are humorous when young, because of the regrettable errors they make in grammar and pronunciation. But the children of tragic people, their suffering illuminates. Their tragedy is much like an inheritance."

"Tough titty."

"We must have the child."

We drove past walls of evergreens, the coastal mountains framing the horizon, moving underneath overpasses and their grassy knolls, yellow and patchy, until we reached the city limits and the highway ended. Richard rolled down the window and let the warm air whip back his hair as he read aloud the signs we passed. "Please report Vanpool violators," he said, chuckling. "Caution when amber lights are flashing." "Now entering a nuclear-free zone." He had a right to be happy, I thought. He was only visiting.

A woman with a large video camera on her shoulder stood before a mirrored wall at the CD superstore. She fixed her hair and thrust her chest forward before aiming the camera at her reflection. A red light flickered on the machine—it was recording. She began speaking in French, Quebec French, into the foam-headed mike in her hand. The woman was short and curvy, with hair the color of pink candy floss. She was wearing a white spaghetti-strap top, emblazoned with a picture of a teddy bear at the center, and a pair of black clamdiggers.

I recognized her. She was Ramona, a VJ for the French-language music channel. She looked younger in person, almost my age, and a little pastier in complexion. I had pretty much lost the French I'd learned from my grandparents, but I knew she was speaking about Urethra Franklin, something about an award. Every third sentence or so, her rapid Québé-cois would stop at a clangorous English expression like "Hot Rocks" or "le soundcheck."

"She's pretty, isn't she?" Marina asked.

She *was* pretty hot.

Marina nodded as though she were reading my mind. "You're right."

"What do you mean?" I asked.

"I can tell you like her."

"I don't like her."

"Liar."

There were a dozen other reporters and cameramen huddled before the stage in a casual, prework way. Richard's press credentials allowed us to get past security. We were to stand off to the side of the stage. Richard's head snaked back and forth in search of his cameraman, until his eyes settled on someone. He sighed with relief—more a yelp, really. He pointed to a man wearing a black leather vest, whose hair was combed over. "There he is," he said, as he excused himself.

We caught the last three songs of the Franklins' set, ending with my mother's recycled voice, which I braced myself to hear. Their version of "Bushmills" was catchy, this was true. I hated it the first time I heard it, but couldn't get it out of my head afterwards. It was a scale-model version of genius, how people could do that—my dad once had such a gift. Of course, half the

Franklins' song came ready-made, sampled. But for everyone else, Helena St. Pierre's voice was background noise. For me, it was the toothache in my heart, the cavity and the filling.

I stood there stunned, as I always did, until roadies—skinny, efficient men wearing ponytails and black jeans, their heads bowed—stepped onto the stage, removing amplifiers and turntables. A long table and microphones were being placed on the stage, which only took up a tiny corner of the store, a complex the size of a warehouse, its ceilings fabulously high, television screens ten feet tall placed above payment counters and the bag check. Urethra Franklin stood in the background talking to a woman with a noteboard and a walkie-talkie. The band consisted of three members. I knew their names from TV: Rob, who was middle-aged and tanned the color of rosewood, played keyboards; Dorit, a round girl wearing Lennon specs, was the drummer; and Hugo, who was of Turkish extraction, his neck long and head shaved so that he resembled a ferret, the rapper with those rhymes about Che Guevara and Michel Foucault. Beside them were two middle-aged native men. One was squat, the other tall, both with thick arms and heavy black hair. The tall one was wearing tinted glasses and a suit, and kept putting a fist to his mouth and coughing loudly. The squat one next to him wore a white jacket and chef's hat, an easy smile on his face—all incisors.

The store had been two-thirds full when we arrived. By now there were people milling outside, not yet allowed to come in, banging against one another anxiously. The crowd inside began to rush the stage, running into security and the reporters already assembled. I was pushed toward the stars onstage. Then

I began pushing myself toward them, toward their foreign smiles. I tugged Marina along with me.

Most of the group's fans were either teenage girls wearing sparkly eye shadow and tracksuits or older men in leather biker jackets. The younger fans brought along their mothers. They wore their hair stylishly, slicked back or highlighted, and took turns peeping at their watches.

One little girl was staring at me.

"Are you native?" She said this with a serious look on her face.

I nodded.

"When I grow up, I'm going to be native, too."

A hyperactive man wearing a Molson Canadian T-shirt and sunglasses was standing among the reporters. As he talked, his elbow caught the girl in her eye. She began to cry silently, her mouth yapping open like a little bird ready to be fed. "Shit," the reporter said. "Shit." He pulled out a twenty-dollar bill from his wallet and tried to fold it into her hand.

"Excuse me."

It was Ramona.

"Like, I need to use the washroom, okay? May I ask you to watch my camera?"

I nodded.

"I can trust you, eh? You look clean. You won't run away with my camera?"

She left me no chance to answer before thrusting the camera at me. It was large and unexpectedly heavy with a leather handle. Then she gave me her microphone, with its spongy head and the French-language music channel's logo on it. Ramona disappeared to the back of the store, running girlishly.

Marina smiled scornfully. "Look at you. Camera Man—he who keeps his eyes trained on the sizzle. Holding the camera for the television personality. I think Frenchy looks a little bloated. She's got an ass the size of a tractor trailer. But, hey, you're the one who's got to live with himself the next day." She made kissing sounds. "Maybe she likes you, Saul. That wouldn't be hard for me to believe. You really do have a knack with the ladies."

"I'm my father's son."

"Ha, ha."

Marina snatched the microphone from my hand and moved in front of the camera, jutting her chest out like Ramona. I aimed the camera at her, watching her through the viewfinder, grainy blue.

"Hello, my name is Jen, Jen Ackroyd from Danbury, Connecticut. I'm honored to have made the quarter-final stage of the preliminary spokesmodel competition. Fucking mind-blowing. Excuse me, can we start the fucking tape again? Here we go again, nimrods. The presentation I'd like to make is about popular music. Unless you're a bloody Mongoloid, you know popular music is good because people around the world like it, and it brings us together. That's why it's not called *unpopular* music. Hello, popularity? See, that's the point. Hello, community? Hello, liberty? Hello, safety from Quaker militias? The band we're talking to today goes by the handle 'U' Franklin. U standing for a part of the body that's, you know, *down there*. Franklin, as in one of our founding fathers. They're responsible for a *rilly* sweet-assed song called 'Bushmills Threnody.' I don't want to ruin anything for you, but it's, like, total *fuck-me* music. They didn't write it, or even sing it. These, like,

Canadians wrote it and sang it, but 'U' Franklin have made it better, because they put drum machines to it and they rap over it. Anyway, I wouldn't recommend listening to music made before 1996—a lot of it was recorded by people who have *now passed away*."

At that moment, a man in sunglasses, the same one who had tried to bribe the little girl, stepped onstage. He began speaking into a headset mike in front of the table. He tapped the microphone before him—a thud came from the PA. An automatic camera whined and snapped as he introduced himself—he was the DJ at a local top-forty station. "How is everyone here today? Yeah, well, swell to hear. I see a lot of students here today. What is this, a professional day? God bless the public school system."

The DJ introduced the band members individually to applause and howls. They assembled on the stage, taking their seats behind the table. I strained toward them. They looked so lifelike. The flashbulbs really began to light.

I saw Ramona behind us, shoving through the crowd, her platform heels clapping against the floor, utter pissed-ivity covering her pretty, round face. She stood on her toes. We were at the side of the stage, and she could barely see over the heads of other onlookers.

She took the microphone from Marina and clamped the camera onto her shoulder, pressing the red record button on the machine.

Rob the keyboardist stood up and said a few words.

"We gratefully accept this award. It is a tremendous honor."

He returned to the table. Reporters began yelling out questions. Rob the keyboardist would point at one of them, and the crowd would struggle, generally failing, to hear the question. The band members would pause and consult one another, then the keyboardist would answer into a mike. And we hung on his every word.

"Yes. Yes. This is true.

"No, we are still looking at scripts. If we see one, we will consider it.

"Yes, Hugo was joking.

"The question concerned our influences. Our parents, the music of your Helena St. Pierre, Marcel Duchamp, your McLuhan, Tarkovsky. We met a taxi driver this week who said that his dental work was paid for by faith in God and his winnings at the greyhound track. He is a purveyor of esthetic bliss and my most recent influence.

"Entirely not.

"We have an opportunity to do this. This is good.

"What you say might be true, but if that were the case, then it has been unintentional, more a realization of dreamlike desire.

"Our dreams are like confetti.

"Completely false."

Rob then urged the two native men onto the stage.

"I must add," Rob was saying, "and we have repeated this many times while here, that we feel especially close to the people from this country. We feel a strong connection to your natural settings, to the authenticity of your native people. We sing that 'property is crime.' We learn that from your native people, especially our new friends." He nodded to the two native men. "Property, the desire to profit from it, threatens every relationship, even as we speak. It saddens us. I speak for the group, completely. We have thus decided to extend our support to our two friends, Ricky and Ezra Sinclair."

The two men announced plans to block a bridge in North Vancouver that Friday to demonstrate an unfair land treaty. Cameras started taping again as they explained how, to publicize the event, they were planning to bake the world's largest quiche in the parking lot of a nearby mall. "People," Ezra said, "have also been unfair to fat. It is a necessary part of a diet."

"One's body exists in the world," Ricky continued, "yet the world lives through the mind."

Cameras starting clicking again, hands were raised, but Ricky and Ezra returned to their places against the back wall.

"One more question," Rob the keyboardist announced.

He scanned the crowd; reporters were waving small tape recorders in their hands. His attention turned toward the side of the stage, his gaze falling on Ramona, who was at the very edge of the stage.

"Tell us your feelings about the death of Helena St. Pierre," Ramona said, before pointing her mike in his direction. "Please speak good English."

"We know only her voice," Rob said. "That being said, we feel that she was murdered by her scumbag husband."

The two native men nodded along in agreement, then Rob thanked us for coming.

My hand fell to my side.

When we returned from the city, Richard and Marina convinced Dad and Louise to come to karaoke night with us. I decided not to argue with them, for they were keen on warbling to prerecorded music with an enthusiasm reserved for one-time affairs. Why not? There was nothing better to do, no other entertainment within a fifteen-minute drive. There was five- and ten-pin bowling, there were waterslides, there was this.

Every Wednesday, they came in jackets and leather clip-on ties and sequin cocktail dresses, sipping Tom Collinses and house-special double martinis, watching their friends and co- workers perform on the sunken stage and black-and-white- checkered dance floor, the disco ball hanging sullen and unused above it. We managed to secure one of the last booths against the brick walls at the Silver and Gold lounge, with plush magenta seats and our very own personal oil lamp, away from the singles swarming around the bar.

Dad and Louise arrived early, and Dad was several glasses into Cutty Sark.

"It's because of that damned song," he said, "that I can't order a glass of Irish whiskey without some drunk serenading me."

A thought crossed my mind. "I bet someone sings that tonight."

I didn't know why it seemed so repulsive, but it did, more than the actual record, German remix or otherwise, could. I slumped in my seat, stomach upset, convinced it would hap- pen, waiting for it to happen. Dad had the same look on his face, ashen and sour. I remembered what Urethra Franklin said about Dad being a murderer, whose actions—the drug use, the domineering behavior, the emotional abuse revealed in the unauthorized biography—somehow inexplicably forced her suicide eighteen years later. I stared at my father, sizing him up, much as I did that morning. He didn't have that much power.

We watched two men singing "Love Shack."

A woman wearing a feather boa singing "Life Is a Highway."

Three brothers in matching tank tops singing "Wild Eyes"
by the Stampeders.

A fat guy singing "Your Cheatin' Heart."

Two hippie girls singing "Shiny Happy People."

Another guy singing "Sweet Caroline."

"You're looking bored," Marina said to me. "You don't want
to be here, do you? I dragged you here, didn't I?"

I shook my head.

Dad sat across from Marina, a slippery smile on his face.
Marina just stared into her drink, playing with her straw.

"I once fell in love with a man while drinking margaritas,"
she shouted over the music. "We were in a pretentious Cuban
restaurant. He said he wouldn't kick me out of bed for putting
ice in my beer." We watched Richard and Andreas singing
Springsteen onstage. She smiled, a rare, unguarded smile that
made me jealous of her memory. "It only lasted a summer. I
liked the way he walked, he walked as though he were in a
wading pool, but there were problems, irresolvable problems."
She paused, lowering her voice. "I was a slut."

Dad went to the bar.

"Do you mind?" Louise said to Marina, once he was out of
earshot. "Or are you intent on giving everyone in the room a
hard-on?"

"I'm not doing anything," Marina said. "He's looking at me."

Louise snorted.

"That's what you said about Henri the architect. I can see
perfectly well, thank you, and I want you to stop it."

"Okay, okay," Marina said. She excused herself from the table.

Richard and Andreas returned to the table after a rendition
of "I'm on Fire."

"Do you like the Boss?" Richard asked us. "He is like bran."

My father came back from the bar carrying two pints of stout. He placed one in front of me.

"Hey."

I nodded, though I kept my eyes from his. He put a hand on the top of my head, then dropped it.

He mumbled something, but gave up on me and sat down next to Louise, his attentions returning to her. She blushed in the watery, amber light of our oil lamp.

Richard tapped me on the shoulder. He clinked his mug against mine.

"I speak to you on Friday," he said.

He drank four pints of ale quickly, emptying the glasses, his cameraman Andreas, who didn't know a word of English, pounding them back alongside him. Richard wiped his mouth with the cuff of his sleeve.

"Let me speak to you Friday," he said as though I hadn't heard him the first time, or would be more inclined to agree if he repeated what he said.

"I have to be at school," I replied. Trying to be helpful, I added, "We've planned a demo to protest censorship on Friday. You can tape that."

"Then Saturday, yeah. On Friday I must tape the large quiche. It must be Saturday."

"It might not be Saturday."

"This is very disorganized," Richard blurted out bitterly.

He clapped twice to get the attention of a passing waitress. She stopped, cupped a hand against her ear like she couldn't hear, and continued on her way. Richard fumed. When the waitress did return, Richard ordered another pint of Kokanee. "In a clean glass, this time," he said. The waitress put forth her frostiest smile and asked me if I wanted something to eat. I ran my fingers across the foggy, vinyl-covered menu and decided to try the jalapeño poppers.

A man with a baritone singing "Staying Alive."

A skinny East Indian man singing "No Time" by the Guess Who.

A woman singing "Two Becomes One."

A man singing "Ohio."

A man singing "It Ain't Me, Babe," the Johnny Cash arrangement.

Louise and my father speaking closely, their hands under the table.

"What do you think, am I insensitive? Do you think I should be in Thailand?" he asked.

"You need to be here," Louise said, wagging her head left and right.

"Do you know how much a fucking ticket costs? Especially if you don't make reservations two weeks in advance?"

"A mint, I'd bet."

My father nodded smugly, and it seemed then, for the very first time, his hatred for Helena St. Pierre really surfaced. Of course, this wasn't true. He had filled a twenty-year-long separation with his empty slights, but it was the first time I looked at him and figured that he probably wished her dead. I felt my face turn red.

Richard and his cameraman slid out of the booth and let me out. I approached the dance floor next to the stage, where Marina was flipping through the song catalogs, sipping a margarita. As I approached the dance floor, flakes of light fell on her like confetti.

"You look angry," she said.

I was angry because it had happened. Someone began singing "Bushmills Threnody," the original arrangement. She was a heavyset woman who occasionally lagged half a beat behind. The stage lights switched from orange to purple. She stood by a prompter, which scrolled out the lyrics across a television screen, the words highlighted in pink as they were sung:

> I try to forget about you
> But you write, you telephone too
> Oh, my dear,
> Your hands so soft
> How can I sleep you off
> Like a hangover from the night before?
>
> I used to see you first thing in the morning
> And the last thing I heard was you saying good night
> So how could you be so cruel?
> When you said I was playing you
> That I've been making you out to be the fool

The crowd held still, all of them aware of recent events, a few even recognizing my father. They kept their eyes fixed on their drinks—including Jana, who had just arrived with Officer Dale and taken a table on the other side of the room, away from Dad and his young girlfriend—as if extraneous movement would further heighten the embarrassment.

I could almost hear Dad start in on his stories about the song. Dad only ever talked about that song. How he wrote it in his room at the Roger Miller King of the Road Motel in Nashville, on tour in support of a second album, nursing a nasty case of stomach flu. How he had to insist on having the song on the record, because Leni, my mother, fresh off another mental breakdown, which saw her hospitalized for three weeks in April 1973, thought the song too sappy and self-pitying. "Sappy? Melodramatic?" my father screamed. "That would suit you fine. That song is you." He laughed at her. And then he promised, if the tune made the top ten, knowing full well it would be a b-side, he'd start a family like Leni wanted, because that was what she had wanted; that was supposed to make her happy and content.

My heart sinking.

My mouth dry. It didn't matter that this woman mumbled off-key and sweated underneath the stage lights. You couldn't go around pretending you were my mother. I wouldn't stand for it. The woman onstage could've been a remarkable singer, and she could've been the most beautiful woman in the world, with a voice like a canary or a skylark or a nightingale, a voice to which poetry aspires, and it wouldn't have mattered. Because Dad was right—Helena St. Pierre was that song. Everyone thought so. Or at least I did. You could sing the same words, but it was a poor impersonation, just like you could put on my mother's clothes, her cowboy boots, her dashiki, her fringe jacket, the white gown she wore on her last tour, the one with the ruffled taffeta collar, but get it completely, perfectly wrong. It made sense that Urethra Franklin sampled my mother's voice.

I left the bar and stood stone-faced outside in the parking lot. I sat in Richard's rental car, ready to leave, sitting out there for half an hour until everybody was willing to go. Dad was right. Every word of it was her, every crack of her voice, every ragged, weary sigh was my mother, who the world knew was dead.

Thursday

The lunch bell sounded and my fellow classmates, in their summer peasant dresses and sandals, their cutoffs and Converse All-Stars, their Tevas, muscle-shirts and pylon-orange track shorts, went outside. They were baring brown and mocha and pasty off-pink and bronze and tawny skin. They began trickling out from classrooms, taking their plastic containers with celery sticks spread with superchunk peanut butter and sprout and feta sandwiches in unlabeled brown bags past the paper and glass recycling bins. They went by the posters advertising the yoga club meetings and the native-style mural painted on a cafeteria wall featuring the raven, the school mascot, so they could eat outside underneath the languorous sun, which rationed its visits to this area.

I was trying to live half an inch under my own skin.

Rose was standing by my locker, reading a book.

"You're not allowed to read that," I said, moving past her,

turning my back toward her as if I were afraid she would steal my locker combination.

"Says who?" Rose said. She put the book into her bag. "My parents say we should be allowed to read what we want."

"Good for them."

I opened my locker, then realized I didn't need anything from it. I already had on my rain jacket, which I always wore until it became too warm to bear. And I certainly was in no mood to study. I shut the locker door and stepped away from Rose. She took hold of my jacket sleeve.

"I tried calling you last night," Rose said.

"Was it important?"

"I just wanted to talk."

"About what?"

"Nothing."

"Well, I'm here. Why don't you tell me now?"

"What if I said I'm pregnant?"

Her chin was bunched and her gorgeous eyebrows knit together. I had upset her, her eyes were set a certain way. She wanted to yell at me, but wouldn't because she was that close to crying. She was wearing a baggy sweater and sweatpants— clothes that she was now starting to fill out again.

I hated her.

"Jesus," I said, yanking my arm away from her, almost reflex-ively. I wanted to take it back, but we stood there, Rose's hand held up in reproach.

"You're not really, are you?" I asked. "Tell me you're not."

She shook her head.

"I'm not," she said.

"Thank you."

She gulped and started breathing heavily as if to calm herself down. "I wanted to talk."

I walked past her, my gray backpack catching against her chin. She winced, putting her hand to her face. I felt helplessly mean, cruel by default.

"People do that," she said.

I turned around and her eyes were wet.

"What?"

"They talk."

I squinted at her angrily, out of exasperation. "That's all they ever do."

The band room, where Navi, Hedda—the anarchist from Olympia, Washington—and I held our lunch-hour walkout information session, was designed like a theater, with terraced levels that ascended from the conductor's podium at the front of the room to the percussion section, its large bass drum and xylophone prominent at the back. I took a seat near the front, where the brass section sat. On the floor was a photocopied flute part for "Mack the Knife." A brown shoeprint was stamped across it. I watched Navi on the podium, his slender shoulders hunched, occasionally halting but gaining momentum as he continued speaking, periodically raising his head from his index cards and smiling brightly at his audience. Thirteen people showed up to hear Navi give his reasons for the planned action: he listed the civil liberties that had been infringed on when our lockers were searched and when students were questioned by policemen, not to mention the book censorship that lay behind the alleged toxic nerve gas threat. He underscored the necessity of direct action. He had done his research and briefly quoted Veblen and Bakunin from lined, yellow index cards.

"In short," he said, before beginning the discussion period, "the discourse of power precludes privacy and free thought."

Navi's oratorical skills were accentuated, perhaps slightly unhinged, by his appearance. In a bow tie and a green velveteen blazer, he fostered the image of a man who had other things on his mind. His hair was slicked back, and even from where I sat, I could smell the Listerine on his breath. This was the same person who one Halloween night as a ten-year-old roamed our misty, amber-lit streets as Orville Redenbacher, popcorn magnate.

Navi: student, photo artist, poet, musician, disruptive element. He liked people and planning events, and had confidence in his own ability to cajole and organize. Before his revolutionary aspirations, there had been team sports like softball and soccer. There had been Hot Dog Day, which he single-handedly revived, and record-setting UNICEF drives. There had been go-karts and video arcades, summer fairs where I'd lose him in flashing lights and stale candy floss and carnival music.

Hedda spoke about making T-shirts that would read, "Frances Brooke Secondary, Inmate # _____" or "Kill Your Inner Cop." Navi wanted publicity. He had called both local dailies and a television station in the city, but had yet to hear back. Hedda had also enlisted something called Rent-a-Mob, a group of university students that came to any protest, given twenty-four hours' notice, ready "to meet all your activist needs." There were plans for a barbecue and a live band, Throws Like a Girl, a straight-edge group at whose squat Hedda was staying. The walkout was to be a community event that extended past the school, where Navi's posters had been taken down an hour after they were posted. I was to re-poster Friday morning and had crowd-control duties during the event. He assigned the responsibilities for new posters to three ninth graders, two girls with nose piercings and hemp wristbands, and another in a bomber jacket and army boots, who encircled him like a pack of lapdogs and spoke in anxious, breathy tones.

"Completely off the topic," I said to Navi, running my finger along his velveteen jacket, "but may I add that you're looking especially spiffy today?"

"Sometimes you have to look your best," Navi said, "to unlock the champion inside."

"You really look as if you deserve a prize."

For the rest of lunch hour after the information session broke up, Hedda, Navi and I sat out on the gray wooden bleachers with other students. Bhangra was playing out of a car CD player in the parking lot behind us, Indian singers accompanied by dance beats. The track and soccer field lay in front of us underneath the deep blue sky, which was dotted with seagulls and lined with narrow wisps of cloud, jagged as shark's teeth. Past it, to one corner at the edge of the school grounds, was a baseball diamond. A waist-high wire-link fence separated the school from generous backyards—from their above-ground swimming pools and swing sets, an occasional trampoline, too.

Hedda was a heavy woman in goth makeup, with shoulder-length black hair that framed her face. She was sweet and weirdly giggly, and she sort of treated Navi and me like we were kid brothers. She brought us lunches, chocolate soy milk in juice boxes and egg-salad sandwiches on crustless whole wheat.

She had driven across the border in a rusty green El Torino station wagon to help us out. On the way here, she picked up a hitchhiker south of Seattle who told her dozens of bad jokes, all of which she related to us. "So a writer is in a car with his mistress," she said. "The mistress is driving. The writer looks out the window, then says to her, 'You're passionate.' 'Oh, how sweet,' the mistress says. 'No, no,' the writer says. 'You're passhing the likkur shtoor.'"

We sat on the bleachers drinking chocolate milk, listening to Hedda's jokes and reading her zine, *Pig Abattoir*. Navi was featured in the latest issue. He had published a poem, "Absence":

> i do not have a cat
> it has no shape no mass no color
> nor a soul for that matter
> it did not act differently after it was neutered
> because i did not have it neutered
>
> i do not have a cat
>
> its meow is indefinable
> it hits eleven and one-half microtones
> in frequencies
> heard by both narwhals and unicorns
> (its forefathers often possessed this meow)
>
> the cat does not scratch out my eyes
> nor does it evoke fond childhood memories

O cat, you do not comfort me
(as better cats do)
but I will label you neither good nor bad

Accompanying the poem was a photo-study entitled "Studies of Absence," comprising six blurry photos of a marmalade-colored cat in a wicker basket. Cats were not allowed in Navi's house on account of his mother's allergies, a situation that brought Navi not a little grief.

"*Pig Abattoir*," Navi said, "has subscribers in New Zealand and the Caribbean."

"It's not a big deal, really," Hedda said. "Not if you get into the right circles. Find conventions, acquire favorable reviews. Meet other people who write letters and trade zines by mail. I'm trying to put it online, but I think it might alienate some of my friends."

"*Pig Abattoir* has three Amish subscribers."

"Avenues of communications are being advanced, while our words—the substance of thought, the currency of imagination—are stripped away from us, by illiteracy and ad copy, because thoughtfulness, discretion, diversity stands in opposition to the profit margin. People opt for corporation-modulated, systematized living situations because they see no choice."

"They give you a choice of Pepsi or Coke, as if those are your only two options. In place of choice, we get a soft-drink binary."

Hedda rolled her eyes and smiled—one of those killer, secret smiles that women deploy strategically, intricate and coy, like a playing card face down. She offered me a mandarin orange. I declined. She ate it herself, ripping into the orange's skin with her long black fingernails. "I hated high school," she said. "I tried killing myself twice in my senior year. I mixed Southern Comfort with my stepmother's Valium. The zine saved my fucking life."

"*Pig Abattoir*'s about being your own spokesperson," Navi said. "Being your own hero. We try our best to reach out to high school kids who'd otherwise find religion—one of those cranky religions."

Our graffiti from two days back was already gone, white-washed over by custodians the following morning. No one had been caught yet.

"What's the damned book about?" Hedda asked.

"It's hard to explain," Navi said. I'm pretty sure he hadn't read it. "You're going to have to read it yourself."

Hedda smirked as if she were daring to call his bluff. "I've got T-shirts to get done for tomorrow."

As I was leaving school, I passed Anders Wong, one hand on his bottle-laden shopping cart, at the pay phone outside the store. Anders kept clicking the receiver.

"I need twenty-five cents," he said. Anders was a stocky man. He was wearing a turquoise turtleneck sweater and an unflattering pair of spandex bicycle shorts. He had an odd odor, though not exactly a bad one—like the way someone's clothes smell after a night around a campfire.

"I've got to call," Anders said. "I see her in my dreams; I see her in the arms of another man. My baby doesn't pick up the phone. My baby's not home. She's with him. She left in the middle of the night. She ran away to be with him, the man who wrote that book. I don't hear her voice anymore."

Anders said he'd been trying to use this phone since nine-thirty.

In the bottom of my trouser pockets I found a quarter. He took the coin, fingering it in his palm, before dropping it into the machine.

"I'm a dangerous man, Saul."

"Why?"

"I have my reasons."

There was the sound of a voice on the other line, distant and gray, then Anders making what I figured to be his usual toxic nerve gas threats.

It was the warmest day of the year, and even as I walked into a breeze, I could feel my T-shirt sticking to the small of my back. I went along Trunk Road until it intersected with the highway, then I took the overpass, which presented the lazy, midday traffic as it passed through our town and the flat, shingled roofs of our houses.

It was written in pink block letters, not on a bed sheet, but on a piece of white tarp fastened with cord: "Helena St. Pierre: 1950–1998." This incontrovertible fact, so harsh and wrong, a matter of public record. The cord was tightly double knotted and difficult to untangle. My hands were raw when the first knot began to loosen. I wondered whether anyone would have expected it to come to this—whether my mother had given much thought to me, whether she had ever imagined me standing here right now.

She was the remarkable half of a minor celebrity couple, her voice a prairie wind in February, when winter settles on the land like an uninvited houseguest on his hundredth night, a native woman who was so shy she would sit alone in a dark room or in a bus for hours before a show, who would beg her husband to cancel tours. On-air tributes to my mother included old film footage from their tour, the big one that followed the success of "Bushmills" in 1974, black-and-white stills from their folk-singing days. Her reclusive nature was underscored—her disappearance after a 1980 Labor Day show, which nearly caused a riot because of a withheld encore.

Her death was like the sound of a stone falling into a well long after it has disappeared.

I folded the tarp into a square and stuffed it into my knapsack.

The cars stopped at the intersection, then I gripped the rail and leaned forward, collecting spit in my mouth for the most contemptible blue BMW 325 in recent memory.

I felt something on the back of my neck, dropping on me. I put my hand to my neck. It felt wet and grimy. I looked above to the seagulls circling forth, going about their business. Business as usual.

Dad and Andreas were in the front room preparing for their interview. Andreas was moving furniture, Dad clipping a microphone to his shirt. "You're going to like this," Dad said to me, staring into his chest. "I'm going to pour my bleeding heart out." He almost cackled. I shrugged my shoulders. Dad had the front room decked out like some shrine. Above his chair on the mantel of his gray-brick fireplace was his Juno Award for "Bushmills" and a picture of Dad sitting at a table in a Greek restaurant with Warren Zevon, the woman who played Bailey Quarters on *WKRP in Cincinnati* and the guy who owned the restaurant. Above these souvenirs was the Gretsch White Falcon, the big hollowbody with a shiny silver whang bar I'd admired as a five-year-old, the same guitar he used on tours and recordings when he wasn't playing his twelve-string. It was mounted on the wall like a large polished fish.

"You should charge admission," I said.

There was a large hole in the front window, which faced the residential street and our shrubbed cul-de-sac. Dad had taped a sheet of cardboard over it with gaffer tape until it could be repaired.

"Dad, you been getting death threats?"

"Why sure," he said cheerfully. "Isn't everyone?"

Richard bounced into the room wearing his makeup. His reddish face was powdered, and there was something girly about his eyelashes—they were curled. He was wearing so much powder on his face that he looked like a bloody mime.

"Yeah, totally radical," he said. "We discuss the music, we establish the time and place through sprightly montage. We play memorable clips, television appearances."

"We'll clear the air with this. People think I'm the Ike Turner of Canada," Dad said. "No one knows what happened. No one fucking cares. It's a native-rights issue; it's a feminist issue. They want to throw bricks and UPS hate mail to my front door. You should see it. I have a stack of angry correspondence piled on my desk. This morning, I had to sign for a box of dog shit. There are people out to get me. I'm not afraid of them—well, there's this one guy."

"Who?"

"There's this large man somewhere who wants to rape me. Either that or shoot me."

"No joke?"

"I don't joke about large men."

Richard's hennaed hair was gelled up into spikes. He was still wearing a white bib over his black silk shirt. On his neck was a small gob of shaving cream. He pointed to me.

"I speak to you tomorrow, is good?"

I shook my head. Richard sighed loudly, then looked to my father.

"Think it over," Dad said. "Say your piece. No one's going to force you to say anything."

Andreas was adjusting a light next to the fireplace. He said something in German to Richard, who nodded.

"It is agreed," Richard said. "We must have the child."

The hallway floorboards creaked as I approached my old bedroom. Across the hall was my dad's room. The walls were thin. When I was still living with my father I could hear every word of his fights with Jana. By that time they stopped caring who was listening. I would stare at the stucco ceiling and the plain white ceiling lamp, round and antiseptic like a urinal cake, the crickets chirping outside my window, the scratchy blue curtains drawn.

Louise lay across my father's unmade bed, napping. A pillow had fallen onto the brown carpet, the white dress Louise wore at the barbecue folded over a chair next to a desk, on which sat Dad's hate mail heaped like a paper pagoda. She was curled up, wearing only a black T-shirt and khaki shorts, her head resting on the underside of her forearm. Her laptop lay open beside her, its screen blue and flickering.

Jana and I had moved out of the house quickly. Jana left all her books, titles like *The Moving Finger* by Agatha Christie, *Play As You Learn Bridge*, *The Essential Gardener*, on the living-room shelves beside the leather-bound encyclopedias, her clothes in the closet and, in a basket hanging in the shower, hair and bath products, conditioner and extra-fancy gels and fruity soaps, which Dad had yet to throw away. We had left the undersized desk from my room, taking only the bed. My posters were still hanging—a map of the world, a hockey poster, a guide to sign language that a man on the street sold me. I looked at my room: it seemed as if I had been waiting for it to be occupied by strangers.

A foldout cot was set up in my room. Marina sat there cross-legged reading Louise's copy of *Baroque-a-Nova*. She put the book down, spine-up on the bed, beside a blue airline pillow and an open sleeping bag.

Louise was still mad at her, Marina was saying, still jealous that she would steal my father.

"She's driving with her emergency brake on, if you know what I mean."

"How is it?" I asked. I sat down beside her, crossing my own legs.

"It's like a Romeo and Juliet story spanning two hundred years of Canadian history. Flashbacks, flashforwards. I get the feeling I'm missing out a lot. Like the use of weather in this novel." She picked up the book and flipped through it. "'It was twenty below at Portage and Main'—page six. 'The snow fluttered down onto rooftops like moths who had tired in their ascent toward the sun'—page twenty-seven. What's the fascination with weather in your country?"

"The typical fascination."

She laughed. She thought this was funny. And I sat amazed at how unpredictably her laughter came, how thin-lipped and deadpan she was until it did. She folded one leg into the other, the wonky metal cot creaking as she got into the lotus position. She was always crossing her legs and moving. I liked that about her.

She stood, in a pair of Converse hightops, five feet six inches. Or just under 168 centimeters. My best guess was that she weighed between 100 (45.5 kilograms) and 130 pounds (59 kilograms). She looked resplendent in a tank top. She smelled like orange Jell-O or peach bubble gum. She liked to use the adjective "wicked," as in "wicked harsh." She was blonde and American, from the northeastern area—her *r*s occasionally flattened, so that "wicked harsh" sounded like "wicked hawsh," and she complained mildly about how funny homogenized milk tasted in Canada. She was grim and sardonical and fucked up—albeit in a mortally attractive way. She appreciated attempts to communicate and behave with authenticity. She listened to the horrible music of my parents, folkies turned rock balladeers, which had seemed very odd but was starting to make sense, or was maybe something I had just accepted because my parents' music, perhaps crass, was sad and stirring. She might be teasing me. Or perhaps she sort of liked me. She'd mentioned last night how she quit smoking pot when she was twelve, because she didn't approve of *that culture*. But she adored margaritas and daiquiris, summer drinks she consumed with a speed and gusto that belied their essential girliness.

All signs would indicate that she was here on earth to make a difficult situation worse—to be the object of a lustful crush,

to distract me from the untimely death of my mother, the
anger I felt toward my father and the ambivalence for my sort-
of girlfriend.

How do you seduce an older woman? I wanted to know this
badly. This was valuable information.

The last image of my mother is of her hand, then a door clos-
ing. During Richard's interview, he plays this for my father on
a fourteen-inch monitor Andreas has set up on a coffee table
between Richard's and Dad's armchairs. Dad is in a buttoned-
up denim shirt and cowboy boots, his silver hair tied in a ponytail. Is he wearing makeup, too? I'm not sure. Richard does his
German spiel, his introductory remarks, addressing the camera
directly. The rest of the interview is in English, to be subtitled
in the future. On the monitor is footage shot recently, of Dad
at home, Dad driving around, Dad playing "Four Strong
Winds" on his Guild. It is the kind of footage you expect to see,
but which seems false and staged when the person shown put-
tering around is your father.

"Where have you been?" Richard asks. And Dad shakes his
head.

Where has he been? He has been hanging around. He has
raised a kid, remarried and divorced again. He has set roots.
There were comeback albums—two of them, and a third
attempt given up halfway through the first recording day, when
he figured his reedy voice would never inspire the hearts of radio
listeners. Of course there was the song for starving Africans—he
sang his one line after Geddy Lee from Rush—there was his one
acting job, the guest appearance on *The Littlest Hobo*, typecast as
a down-on-his-luck musician befriended by the Hobo, Canada's

Lassie, a guileless, slack-jawed German shepherd. There were small club dates with other female singers. There was a jazz vocalist who owned a dozen boas, a big-haired Texan who flew in because she had dreamed lucidly about playing with him on an all-lavender stage, a twenty-year-old in leg warmers who hopped on the *Flashdance* wagon a week too late. He was *reinventing his sound*. He was *devoting time to a couple of projects*. But his success was contingent on her voice, the voice of a woman he ran into one night in May 1969 after a gig, whom he saw a month later across the street, buying cantaloupe at the first organic grocer in the neighborhood. He chased her down. "Knowledge through pleasure," she said on their first date, wondering if there was a bumper sticker she could find with this written on it. "People don't get it." Of course she didn't have a car, but she could stick it on anybody's bumper. Property is a crime. "Do you know the human body can last forty days without food?" she asked at a Moroccan restaurant. My dad's eyes narrowed. This woman, who had broken up with her boyfriend, was already dating Ned the painter and Hayden who liked ceramics and some guy who etched. But I'm the guitarist, he must have thought, because, in his quiet, unassuming manner, he sort of overwhelmed the competition. I'm the dick artist.

He says, "Richard, Richard, where have I been?" He runs his hand over his hair. There is a hiss in his voice, the bile rising. "Don't even start, Richard."

Richard has a small remote control that he uses to run the video clips. There is early performance footage. Dad in a serape and flares. Helena St. Pierre in an orange dashiki.

"I was never comfortable as a folkie. It wasn't me. Show business was performance. It wasn't supposed to be *art*; it wasn't

intended to be *truth* or personal revelation, because, from what I
knew, those things were unpleasant. It was something you saw
or heard, something you went to, that made you happy and
entertained you, so you could get through another day at the
salt mine without having a go at your foreman with a pickax, so
you could go home and not slap your wife and kids. You performed to entertain, not to confess, not to sing about your
childhood. You performed because you wanted to be part of
something beautiful. I got into music because I wanted to wear
a tuxedo like Peter Lawford, my hero. I made my father jealous,
because he always wanted to be the performer. He would drink
and sing in the morning and cut hair while hung over. I was
cruel to my old man. You can rebel against your parents, but it's
always on their terms. They say to you, 'This is how you can
destroy me,' they hand you a knife and then point to their weak
spot, and then you either do it or you don't."

Concerning the performance footage:

"This came about a year after Leni and I met—we knew
friends who were supposed to play, but their drummer was
stricken with appendicitis two nights earlier. It was for a city
television station that wanted local content. I don't remember
this taping very well. Only that a cameraman fainted. Of
course, this was her doing. She used to make them all faint.
Not just girls and swishy little men. But big burly bikers even,
who would come to our shows so they could swoon like women
at the feet of, you know, Peter Lawford. Later on, she learned
how to sing without incurring casualties. She held back."

He holds up a finger, then reaches in his pocket. "Just a sec,"
he says. Richard lights his cigarette.

"I knew people. There were people to be known. You meet

this guy who chants William Burroughs aloud in pig Latin, you stay at this person's girlfriend's loft and studio space, she makes hats out of felt on the side, she knows another guy who plays tabla, so you form a band. This certainly doesn't happen anymore. People don't know one another. I feel sorry, really sorry, for young kids today. We had fun, more than our parents did, more than our kids ever will. My parents certainly didn't enjoy their lives. They were very sad people, especially after my older sister died. Claudette died of polio. It turned my mother, especially, into an atheist. She cursed God in the morning under her breath, scrambling eggs. They complained that we had it so easy. But we did; we were always fucking around. Cigarettes were cheap, cars were cheap, excessive European vacations were cheap. This was a few years before everybody started choking on their vomit—that cruel winter of asphyxiation, 1971. And the music was more interesting, maybe because we were stupider then—we were pompous—but at least we dreamed in grand and obscene terms. Even Toronto, if you can imagine, was like that, so much as Toronto could be like that. It was as though the town had been built on dirty thoughts. Everywhere. Not just the coffeehouses. They were starting up universities left and right, Marshall Plan dollars from the States or something, and they were letting boneheads teach, true weirdos, but these guys were interesting. You might not have learned a whit about Chaucer, but you were given the chance to see a hung-over English prof up close, railing about macrobiotic nutrition and tantric sex. Not that I ever took a university course, but that's what I hear. I don't know, am I rambling?"

"We have a one-hour show," Richard says.

"You could tell how good a time it was because we dressed like fools. We were deep-sea diving so far up our own assholes that we neglected to observe our glaring dumbness."

"Tell me about her."

"She was crazy."

"Is that all?"

"Come on."

He is sucking his cigarette.

"Of course, everyone knows about this. But, sure, allow me to refresh the public consciousness. Leni was already notorious at the time. She was posing nude for a class, and one of the students—some guy she knew at the co-op gallery—asked whether he could paint her on a street corner. Downtown Toronto. It would be an event: nudity for peace, art for peace. It was as though peace was something you bought at the deli with your coleslaw. She got into a lot of papers, black bars across her tits—you know, use your imagination. She was arrested for that, fined, then she went out and did it again. This time she was spread out on a couch. I went to that one, everyone did. A naked woman lounging on a divan and no cover charge. She was the most beautiful woman I had ever seen, I grant her that. You met Indian people, yeah right. Everybody those days had an Indian grandmother. Newborn children were being named after entire tribes. Cherokee, Dakota, Cree. But you could tell she was the real deal. She was a tiny rail-thin creature, but when she looked in my direction—those eyes—I was swallowed alive, the way a snake swallows a goat, the way fat people slurp up fettuccine in white sauce. There she was in front of the Bay display window, in front of the mannequins. Leni, the performance artist with a

sign around her neck that read, 'Invisible Mink Coat: $1,000.'
This was considered revolutionary. Now they hire malnour-
ished teenagers to do it on billboards. Back then, people threw
dollar bills at her. They hooted. I might have hooted—who
knows? I think her boyfriend threw a punch at me.

"I met Helena Sinclair, I met Leni at a show months later. A
friend invited her to see me play. I shook when she approached
me; I shuddered in anticipation: she looked better with clothes
on. By then, the nudity had lost its novelty. There was a
woman in Ottawa who had set up a naked kissing booth for
peace. Nudity was old. She'd needed something new. She figured all the art she was doing was short-lived. The new art was
all about saying, 'Look at this, look how this is art. And if you
don't think it's art, that it's gorgeous, then you should be looking differently, you patriarchal fool, you establishment lackey
who'll never be loved or appreciated, may your cock drop off
your body from neglect.' But, the thing was, people get tired of
being told where and how to look. It was like church. Who
wants to be in church?

"I asked her how she enjoyed the show. She made a face. I
wasn't much of a singer, she told me. She was never good at
hiding how she felt. She was shy, shy in an aloof, snooty way
perhaps, only because she was afraid to let it be known,
though she did eventually, that she sang. That's the differ-
ence between talent and genius, folks. Apparently, I wrote
well enough. My songs were good, if my singing wasn't. She
wanted to know whether I would write her a song. When I
saw her next, about a week later, I had written the entire first
album. It went well. We played. Who knew she had that
voice? Who knew she was that good? My prayers were

answered. I took her to dinner afterwards because the girl looked like she needed a meal.

"We played our first show soon afterward. It went well and they asked us back. At our next show, someone came backstage and asked me whether we wanted to make a record. Allan something or other, who wore penny loafers with his flares and worked at the record company as the hip talent guy." He snaps his fingers and smiles. "It happened that fast.

"*Blind River* was recorded quickly, almost live in the studio, just minor overdubs, in a dump, in a room lined with purple egg cartons on Yonge Street with an engineer named Lefty. It was more a demo than a record. The name of the group was the St. Pierres, even if we weren't married yet—not for another four months. She said it had a ring to it. Hint, hint, pun, pun. This was about the time that government agency, the CRTC, instituted quotas of Canadian music, so our stations would promote homegrown talent. To qualify, your songs had to be written by Canadians, the music played by Canadians, recorded in Canada and produced by a Canadian. You needed two of those four criteria. Or something like that, I forget. Radio stations loved us, simply because we weren't terrible. I won't speak ill of anyone, no names, but the Cancon rules let a lot of shit slide by. Spectacular mediocrity. We were just a good group at the right time, and the legislation helped us out. Period. Well, maybe, we added some harmonium, we sweetened the songs with strings. Because that sells. Sold.

"So we did well, and she seemed happy enough. She liked playing in front of her friends. For our first show, she mailed rainbow-shaped invitations to her TM class. And though she wouldn't have said it, she was as ambitious as anyone. She wanted the love of the world, but she didn't know what to do with it once she had it. She wanted to return it, I think; she wanted to give it back. She complained when we started making money. She wanted to give it away. Give it away. We argued about that. And then there were hospitals—two times. I don't know what they did, but it was a waste of money no matter which way you slice it. The doctors said there wasn't anything wrong with her. They sat with her in a room and asked her to talk, to talk herself to sleep, because they thought she was suffering from insomnia. You don't just quit; you don't walk away. There lay our differences. I couldn't stop working. I wrote every day. I woke up at six with my Guild and—"

"About your wife," Richard says.

"Of course, of course. That's what you want to know."

The camera is square on his face. He scratches his nose.

"I don't know what to say about her death. It's sad, I suppose, but I was surprised, really, that she survived as long as she did. She heard voices. There was something wrong with her."

"Tell me more."

"If I saw her now, I would say, 'Hello, how are you? Didn't we have a good time?' Then, 'See you. Goodbye.' Why she ran out at the Labor Day show with half a tour to play, another twelve dates, I still don't know, won't ever know, don't want to know. We were professionals. So what if she was under stress, that I knew—she saw another doctor about that; he put her on a prescription. Maybe I'm past caring. I wouldn't have any questions. Why bother? Maybe she'd ask me how I've been. She ran out on our son, left him for me to raise. If we met, I would hope she'd ask me about him."

Richard chooses this precise moment to play the last image

of Helena St. Pierre. The camera shows a crummy apartment
courtyard from high above, where wet clothes hang on lines
stretching from one side of the building to the other. It proceeds unsteadily, past barefoot brown children, following
Richard as he passes a row of orange doors and barred windows.
Richard stops and knocks. A door cracks open, then a hand
crowds the screen. She cries.

The voice of Helena St. Pierre asks, "What are you waiting
for?"

And then the tape stops. There is no more. Richard
switches off the monitor.

This is witchcraft, I think, death crawling toward me on
hands and knees, frame by frame.

Jana wanted me home for dinner. Maybe she thought it strange
that I was spending so much time around Dad, given the situation. More than a year had passed since we'd moved out,
abruptly and bitterly. I remembered hearing the phone ringing
late that night, my father's rumbling. Then Dad and Jana
began to argue. Dad landed one backhanded slap on Jana that
left a bruise along her cheekbone. I woke up that night and
opened my bedroom door to find Dad standing in the hallway
in a white T-shirt and pyjama bottoms, his eyes set on Jana. I
remembered disgust whelming in my heart, looking away from
his face to the floor and the graying hair on his toes, his red
flip-flops. I lost all faith in him after that.

We moved out the next day. Jana said she wasn't afraid of
him, only that things were getting so bad that they had
stopped talking, that it wasn't worth it anymore. We stayed
with Gord and Nadine before we found our townhouse in a

complex that sat placidly beside a nursing home and a children's playground. Dad paid half the rent. Jana had recently finished a degree in history after a ten-year break from school. She had to work, so she put in three or four days a week as a temp. She answered phones and took dictation in large offices full of people who took pains not to learn her name. She would be gone once the regular secretary recovered from the flu or got back from Reno. "It seems like my lot in life—to fill in," Jana said then, lying on the living-room couch with a comforter up to her neck. About that time I dropped out of school, so we spent a lot of time together, just the two of us on the couch watching daytime TV and feeling glum. She taught me to foxtrot to scratchy Django Rheinhardt LPs, and we would dance in the living room, stopping mid-song to move the glass coffee table.

Then one afternoon she told me to get up. It was a big day for both of us, she said. I got showered and dressed. Jana was waiting to go, looking better than she had since the separation. She led me to her car and drove me to school, where, in spite of my weak-willed protests, I re-enrolled in classes. She took me downtown to a salon beside the fish-and-chip house and had her hair highlighted. She forced me to get a manicure.

She had a date that night. With Officer Dale, whom she'd met at the dry cleaners. I remembered the smile on her face, and I knew then how much I depended on her, and how I could say anything to her. Afterwards, we bought fish and chips wrapped in cones of newspaper, and ate in the car. I asked her there, for the first time, about my mother, whom everybody knew but me. I remembered feeling very conscious of my beautified fingernails.

Jana told me my mother announced one day she was leaving
Ian so she could be alone.

She said she was meeting an old lover, this fellow who had
jilted her in Toronto ten years before.

"I told her," Jana said, "that that was no good reason to walk
away from anything."

My mother didn't have a better answer.

From Jana's narrow kitchen with the glazed, red-tiled floor
came the smell of roasted potatoes and curried chicken. Jana
was at the counter, next to the breadmaker, wearing a pair of
thick ceramic bracelets, which clicked together as she tossed a
salad. On the radio was the maritime fiddle music that made
her homesick. I wrapped my arms around her from behind and
kissed her soft cheek. It felt powdery and cool. She smiled
faintly and asked me to set the table. The kitchen table was
cluttered with newspapers, mail and two bowls caked with
dried-out muesli and milk at the very bottom.

"I have news."

"I hate suspense," I said.

She leaned back against the counter, tight-lipped, her eyes
twinkling.

"Dale asked me to marry him."

"So, what did you say?"

"Maybe, I told him. Probably. He wants to start a family, he
says. Your dad never wanted kids with me."

"Oh. Congratulations."

"Dale likes you, Saulie."

"When are you getting married?"

"Not for a while."

"Good."

Jana started clearing the table for dinner, stacking the news-papers for the recycling bin.

"This place is a mess," Jana said.

"We need a maid," I said, something I instantly regretted. I'd opened myself up to reproach. I began arranging the mail in a separate pile on a chair, then scraping off the gunk from the cereal bowls into a wastebasket and rinsing those selfsame bowls in the sink. I was doing my helpful-stepson imperson-ation because I was expecting Jana to lay into me, to say I was an incontrovertible slob and that she wasn't my housekeeper—this performance notwithstanding. But instead she sighed, a tired look seeping from inside out to her face.

"We need a bigger kitchen," I said.

"Maybe."

"Does Dale have a big kitchen?"

Jana sighed again. "Not really."

The timer sounded and Jana pulled the potatoes out of the oven. She poked at them with a fork and wrinkled her nose.

"And your father's finally rebuilding *his* kitchen."

"He had a change of heart."

Jana set the salad on the table. I brought the potatoes from the counter, the hot Corningware scalding my bare hands, and sat down.

"How long has he known this woman?"

"About a week, I guess."

"Hm."

"They wrote him a letter."

"They?"

"She has a friend with her."

"What kind of women would shack up with a middle-aged man after writing a letter to him?"

"The same kind who would run away and join his band when she was seventeen."

Jana clucked in a dismissive way.

"I was never *in* your parents' band. Besides, that doesn't make what she did right. But I suppose you've made your point. Your father is not without his charms."

"There's a large man who wants to rape him."

We sat down and ate, quietly at first. Jana told me Rose called.

"She's a sweet girl, don't you think?"

I nodded.

Jana frowned. But I knew she'd be displeased if she found out how badly I was treating Rose, so I said nothing. She pouted, something she was not above doing when she didn't get her way. I changed topics instead, telling her about the interview and our glimpse of Helena St. Pierre. "It seemed funny that Richard found her, when even Dad hasn't had a clue in twenty years."

"Well, you know, they've got satellites," Jana suggested. "Cold War spy technology."

"Oh, come on," I said. "Please."

"I'm not saying they used Cold War spy technology to find her, just that they could; they have the capability."

"Sure."

"Well, maybe they hired a detective. That sounds credible, doesn't it? A detective."

"A gumshoe. A private dick."

"*Saul.*"

"That's what they're called, *Jana*."

"Fine."

We sat quietly. As another fiddle song faded out on the radio, I added, "Watching Dad interviewed reminded me what a public dick he is."

"*Saul*."

After dinner, I helped Jana with the dishes. I covered the leftover potatoes in plastic, put the leftover curry chicken in containers, and then took a dishtowel and dried by the sink next to Jana, who rinsed and scrubbed plates and juice glasses left over from the past week. Jana asked about school, hoping to find a topic for peaceful dishwashing conversation—the dishes needed to get done. I mentioned the nerve gas scare, how Navi and I responded with his walkout. Jana giggled. She liked Navi. She thought him polite and sweet, his enthusiasm endearing. Navi was the type of person who had half-hour conversations with one's stepmother about gardening and orthopedic footwear. Navi was a big suck.

"What I like about him," she said, "is how he can turn everything into an event—in a good way, though."

"Some crank phoned in the threat over a book."

"What book?"

"*Baroque-a-Nova*, by Nathan Shaw."

Jana turned off the faucet and set her plates down beside the sink. Her eyes narrowed.

"It's been a long time since I heard his name."

The tarp, when unfolded and spread out, more than covered my bed. It extended over the twin-size mattress and hung off the edges. My fingers traced the words "Helena St. Pierre:

1950–1998." I sat at the edge of my bed, imagining her hands on the rail and then one foot over, a pale calf exposed as she straddled the rail, her stomach puckering, the other foot going over. The air smelling smoggy and foreign to her, as it did before she'd gotten used to it—like car exhaust, incense or skewered meat.

The light in the room was off. I lay down on the bed, wrapping the tarp around me. I closed my eyes and imagined the same woman screaming at Richard to go away—I tried to think of her at that moment jumping.

In her periphery, the balconies of her immediate neighbors and those next to them, their woks sizzling and their appliances whirring and blaring, loudly eating electricity from 220-volt outlets. In front of her, the ever-smoggy sky covering the mid-day urban sprawl like a tent made of tightly sewn strips of gauze.

Friday

That morning I flipped through Leslie Erickson's *The St. Pierres Story*. I kept it underneath my mattress, secretively as though it were pornography or samizdat, contraband. I placed it on my nightstand next to Nathan Shaw's book.

According to my parents' unauthorized biography, Helena Sinclair was born in central British Columbia on a Shuswap reserve near Williams Lake, and lived with her maternal grandmother in an unpainted government-built house. Her father had shot himself a week before she was born. A year later, her mother married a white man in Prince Rupert and was, as these stories go, never to be seen again.

Your mother at your age, younger, her skin spotty, eyes squinty but gleaming, her face baby-fat pudgy. Helena is slender with soft hands and a shy smile. She runs her tongue along her bottom lip. She wears pigtails, lipstick and a knotted scarf around her neck—in the style of the

Italian starlet from a film magazine she lifts off a nun at
school. The other girls are afraid of her. They can't ignore her:
she runs around in the yard wildly, ignoring everyone. She
climbs trees at night to be alone. It's like she's sort of possessed, bad luck. And the boys, their waists narrow, their
intentions transparent, all greasy-headed, *blech*, they don't
even rate a mention. They want her, and she lets herself be
had occasionally, just for kicks, although she prefers the company of older men. She makes eyes at her high school history
teacher, the only lay teacher at the school, the only male. It's
fun, it enhances self-esteem, it helps her perfect her walk.
Glide, sway, flick your hair. Cover your mouth when you
laugh. She meets him on a bank off a hunting trail, carrying
an army blanket in her folded cashmere arms, her hair dark
and straight and slick.

You think of your mother in positions of weakness.

The history teacher takes her to Vancouver. And she works
in the diner of the downtown Hudson's Bay Company department store. This woman is too beautiful. And she's an Indian.
Sexy, demure, though maybe a little off-kilter. She doesn't talk
and she doesn't spend time with the other girls in the store.
She hums to herself.

A manager notices her while she's serving him a chicken
pot pie. She smiles meekly because the crust's burnt. Soon
thereafter, he makes the one bold decision of his career and
awards her a scholarship and places her on the "fashion council." She takes it, of course, because what good is physical
beauty if she doesn't use it while she has it, while men still find
her alluring and plausibly innocent, to advance in the world, to
win friends and security, to ward off her bad luck.

They give her a green blazer with a "Bay Fashion Council" badge stitched on the breast pocket. Local models arrive Friday afternoon to discuss hygiene, poise and posture. She's the only native among them. The manager has taken a chance on her, like some test-tube experiment for the new cultural mosaic of the coming years. Her craphole apartment is deemed "unseemly," so the store billets her in the home of an appliance salesman ten months away from retirement. They cap her teeth and teach her to model swimwear. They offer to pay the tuition for a degree in commerce, so that she can be the next generation of cosmetic-counter manager.

Welcome to 1967.

Your mother works at the perfume counter Mondays to Thursdays from eight a.m. to five p.m., and Saturdays from ten to four, offering samples of blush and mascara beside the cash register. This would be enough to bore anyone to thoroughly gushy tears, but then there's the issue of the high school teacher, who wasn't the grand idea she was hoping it to be, either. He's older than she thought, his body unappealing, and he farts wickedly.

It's too much one day at work. She's ready to write her grandmother to wire her bus fare home. In the store that day, the Oriental with the taped-together hornrims and the toque with the earflaps, the creep who's been hanging around her section the past month, is trying to steal a five-ounce bottle of Chanel. She trains her eyes on him like she's taught, until he puts the bottle back on the counter and vanishes behind the Barbour rain jackets in menswear.

Two hours later, he returns, hiding behind a mannequin, spinning the tie rack to the tinkly music and soft lighting. She catches his reflection against a mirrored pillar. He approaches—oh, God, what a dope in his bearskin vest, in his flares—how fast can security get here—in his hair that flicks out like Mary Tyler Moore on *The Dick Van Dyke Show*. He drops something on the table and leaves.

It is a slim collection of poems, Jacques Prévert's *Paroles*, the City Lights edition. She opens the book. As an inscription, someone has written, "You're so cool!"

What does she do? Your mother narrowly averts being caught stealing, leaving work early that day, quitting. Her manager, a smile on her as stiff and frosted as her beehive, asks her where she's going. She smiles back at her and walks away. Your mother, eighteen years old, will move to Toronto, where this funny-looking man seeks to write his novel.

Glide, sway, flick your hair.

She sees him on the street outside the Bay. She fingers the bottle of Chanel in the pocket of her purple faux-fur jacket. The store is about to close, so a guard has to unlock the heavy metal door for her and hold it open.

He isn't your father, just the love of your mother's life.

According to Jana, my mother didn't say too much about Nathan Shaw. He wrote books, she told her. They went East together. He was the one who had saved her from department-store drudgery.

Jana said she met Helena St. Pierre in July 1980. Jana was seventeen years of age and not yet a high school graduate. The St. Pierres had begun a four-month tour that would see them play forty-two large concert halls throughout the continent. It was an ambitious jaunt organized by Ian, who wanted their latest record to crack platinum. His wife had given birth six months ago and already they were back on the road, their child left back with his parents. Jana was handed a backstage pass during the Halifax concert and managed to stay with the band when they took off the next day, flashing half a smile and promising a road manager good karma if she could catch a lift. She wanted to leave the Maritimes, perhaps for Phoenix, where she had a cousin, or San Francisco or Vancouver. Anyplace west. People there were more relaxed about things; all the great things were happening there. She had a feeling she was born ten years too late, but hoped she hadn't entirely missed the good vibes. She met Gord, the pedal-steel player, on her second night. He was sweet and laughed a lot, so in keeping with times past, she decided to be his girlfriend the same way someone chooses toothpaste.

She was lucky. Gord was a sweet man. He kept her away from the road manager and his porno thoughts. He warned her never to touch any equipment and to stay out of the way. That was fine with her. After the first few nights, she decided not to attend the after-show parties, filled with coke and hash and guest-list flotsam—what she could only assume to be the typical assortment of weirdos, industry people and sucks. At the heart of all the action was Ian St. Pierre, a man with heavy eyebrows and rounded shoulders, who managed to be simultaneously menacing and sickly, his face puffy and red from scotch in a powder purple tuxedo shirt. He would glare at her, those eyes in their own way as striking as his wife's. Like Clint Eastwood's movie-star stare down, but more sinister, less heroic, shorter. And even if he dressed and acted like a variety-show parody of the gadfly, she felt him looking at her from the pit of her stomach, from behind her knees. She slunk around the buses during sound checks, talking to the local security people and ballroom cocktail waitresses, smoking Gord's Rothmans in the alleys behind the concert halls, hoping to avoid him.

Jana watched Helena St. Pierre sing twenty-nine times during the tour, every single performance ending with a rendition of "Bushmills Threnody." Ian was obliged to play it, though its success was embittering. For even if he were right and he wrote twenty other tunes as good as "Bushmills," he failed to convince radio stations and record buyers of that fact. By the second week of the tour, he made the touring band rush through the song at one and a half times the tempo of the recorded version, just to get it over with. Somebody joked that the song would soon be renamed "Bushmills Polka."

The band would return for the encore, the stage dark except for a single spotlight on Leni, who stood there teetering, her hands flapping.

Jana thought she was gorgeous, striking and aloof onstage, and that she would live her entire life twenty times over without seeing anyone more beautiful, more lonely, enchanting and sad. She seemed oblivious to the crowd, yet she'd turn away like she heard something, someone calling her.

Last night, Jana spoke, reluctantly at first, of how Helena St. Pierre confided in her during that last tour after they watched cartoons on the luxury tour bus. They'd watch *Bugs Bunny* and *The Flintstones*, and my mother would cover her mouth with her long fingers, the nails chewed off from backstage anxieties, and laugh—the only time, my stepmother claims, that she did. She laughed once for five whole minutes, until her face was purple and Jana was about ready to holler for help, before she said, "Jana, have they hurt you much?"

"Who?"

"Men."

Men who love your mother.

Jana watched them. Ian and Helena. At a state fair, behind a trailer, holding hands, the scent of horse manure from a nearby petting zoo wafting in the humid air. A portable generator buzzing, some megaphone announcement rumbling. It is three hours before the show that night. Just a couple of trailers down, some of the guys in the band are playing pickup floor hockey with roller skates, a few sticks, an egg-shaped ball of gaffer's tape for a puck and orange pylons for nets. Ian kisses Helena's forehead, puts one hand inside her shirt, and presses it flat against her belly.

Ian is not a tall man but he rests his chin on her head.

Or at an airport:

Leni, in her dark glasses, on Valium, heels dragging against the floor. Ian leading her by the elbow to the baggage claim. Maybe she's having a sulk. Maybe it's because she doesn't eat much. Jana's never seen her finish a meal. Leni nibbles.

She jerks her arm away from Ian like a willful rag doll. Ian continues walking maybe ten feet, then turns, waits for her to catch up. Leni seems to look past him, a wobbly smile on her face. She sways, then drops to the floor and begins shaking. Ian crouches beside her, holding her shoulders down to the ground.

A seizure. She hasn't had one of these in three years, Ian says, not since her last visit to the hospital. He sounds more irritated than alarmed, treating it like a temper tantrum.

In concert:

He's terrified that this woman can do this to him, that he dies with every dip and swoon of her voice. He is watching Leni, his jaw to his knees, his eyes rounded. His love for her is territorial, like a prospector guarding his stake, his plot, four invisible lines marking the extent of his longing.

On the road:

Ian likes the fact that Leni has a friend, that she and Jana are up watching television together and talking late into the night. Leni has no friends. She's scary, or so everyone has you thinking.

He knocks on Jana's door one night in Baltimore and thanks her for "keeping Helena calm."

"It's my pleasure," Jana manages back.

Leni's knitting needles click as cartoons flicker on the set in the hotel, the two of them sitting, feet up, on a bed in Gord's room. Leni catches Jana from the corner of her eye and smiles.

She talks as though there's someone sleeping in the room, as though she's afraid to wake them up.

Ian and Gord are downstairs in a nightclub or on a producer's boat. Somewhere with music, a great selection of liquor, a vegetable platter—where there's women and coke. According to Leni, Ian's more of a drinker—when he drinks, that's all he really wants to do—but he plays along. Leni used to party with them on the first couple of tours as her way of relieving stress, but all the rum and Cokes gave her stomachaches. And

liquor is fattening, anyway. If she drinks, it's vodka or gin—
something clear. She decided the parties were the worst part of
touring. That's what she learned from the psychiatrists.

"Am I ruining your night?" Helena asks Jana. "Wouldn't you
rather be at the party? With Gord?"

Jana shakes her head. "I'm tired," she says.

"Ian was looking for you."

"Why?"

"He wanted to know where you went, silly."

"Oh," Jana says. Their bed faces a dresser mirror, which is
next to the television. She sees herself blushing.

"Do you like being here, on the road?"

"I guess."

"You can go home anytime you want. You know that,
don't you?"

"I know. I talked to my parents last week."

"What did you say?" Leni asks.

"My parents, you see, I don't know," Jana says. Leni smiles,
almost motherly. As waifish as she may look, as badly put
together as she can be, Leni's still thirteen years older than
Jana. "They're really nice, but they think I'm too young to be
away. They think I don't know what I want."

"What do you want?" Leni asks, putting down her knitting.
She's making her little boy a red scarf.

"I don't know," Jana says, then starts giggling. She sounds
even younger, like a kid talking with candy in her mouth. I must
stop laughing like this, she thinks to herself. But she doesn't ask
these kinds of questions, Jana thinks, not usually. "I sort of want
to be away for a while. I like being around the band. I like being
around you and Ian."

"Do you want to sing?"

Jana looks Leni square in the eyes, afraid this is some joke, that she's about to burst into laughter.

"No," she says.

"Is it because you don't think you can sing?"

"I have an ugly voice," Jana says. In fact, she used to sing in a choir. She has a fine voice. "You're the one who can sing. You sing beautifully." It takes courage for her to say this to Leni's face, because she's wanted to say it since their first conversation, but didn't lest Leni find it embarrassing or think her another groupie or band hag. And the more she has gotten to know Leni, the wiser she thinks that decision is, but now she goes temporarily imprudent and blurts out her admiration. Leni smiles abashedly, as though an embarrassing secret has been let out. "I cry when I hear you sing. My heart breaks when you sing."

"We'll give you a tambourine," Leni says.

"I don't think I can play tambourine."

"What do you want, then, sweetie?"

The cartoons end. Leni clicks off the TV.

I told her what I wanted, Jana thinks, that I wanted to be here. Maybe Leni wants me to say something else.

The room goes quiet.

"Maybe I don't want anything," Jana says. "I just like being here."

"You might grow tired of it."

"I guess."

"Sometimes I get tired of it," Leni says. "I think maybe I'd be happier if I were by myself."

"With Ian?"

"Don't you ever want to be alone?"

"No." Jana says this without thinking. "I'd rather be with you."

Leni laughs.

"You're a lot like Ian. Ian can't stand being alone either."

Jana sees her reflection, burning again. She moves over to the edge of the bed and sits away from Leni.

"What is it?"

"I don't think he likes me," Jana says. "He doesn't say much."

"Of course he likes you. He likes you a lot."

"Did he tell you that?" Jana asks, feeling a flutter in her chest. She feels treacherous, considering who she's talking to.

"I'm his wife," Leni says, as if to remind her. "He doesn't need to tell me everything."

"I get the impression, you know, that he doesn't." Then she adds, "I mean, I like him."

"You do, don't you?"

"I guess."

"You love him."

Jana starts to apologize: "I'm sorry. I didn't mean—I love you, too. I wouldn't do anything."

She throws her arms around Leni. It's like hugging a hat rack.

"I know you wouldn't."

"I'm sorry."

"I'd like to be alone for a while," Leni says.

"Oh," Jana says, and makes to leave the room.

"I want to get away."

Jana asks where. She stands by the door, not sure whether she should leave.

"I haven't decided yet. I think Ian will be lonely without
me. I think he'll be unhappy."

"I'll miss you, too."

"No, you won't. You'll be with him."

Leni resumes knitting. Needles clicking.

As noon approached, it seemed unlikely any crowd would
assemble on the soccer field. A lack of excitement was dis-
cernible as the young men and women in my English 12 class
hit the Off buttons of their cellphones, clicked shut their three-
ring binders, kept hip-hop beats with their fingertips on slanted,
tortoise-shell-finished desks and with their sandals and sneakers
on the burgundy floor, and snapped shut tubes of fluorescent
mango-orange lipstick to the sound of the third period bell, a
recorded bleep, solid and unremarkable, playing over the PA.

Outside on the soccer field was one middle-aged man.

I saw Navi's head pop into the classroom as we watched the
last hour of *The Handmaid's Tale*.

"The whole third floor had to be postered," he said as we
moved through the hallway.

"I forgot," I said. "I'm sorry."

"Oh, well. Fuck, whatever."

We were both glum about the turnout. I watched two, four,
ten, fifteen students leaving their classrooms, moving with us
to the soccer field. The floor squeaked as we walked.

He had a walkie-talkie, not some toy, but a professional
deal, a rental. I heard Hedda's voice coming from it, staticky
and distorted.

"Proceed with Rent-a-Mob," Navi said into it. "Over."

The intention was street theater, a counter spectacle. Underneath the overcast sky, on the bleachers before the soccer field, sat Hedda, wearing a tiara made of aluminum foil, a huge costume-issue ruby necklace and a strapless ball gown, maroon and crushed velvet, with a sash across it reading, "Miss Police State 1998." She held at her side a bullhorn, which she handed over to Navi, who proceeded to direct the thirty-five members of Rent-a-Mob in the middle of the field. Navi, in his bow tie and tuxedo shirt, looked underdressed. There were two or three men in dog collars, two women with neon-blue hair, a man wearing a rubber Pierre Trudeau mask, a woman with a "Take It Sleazy" T-shirt. They held signs carrying abusive slogans, some with no apparent political content, like "Eat My Ass." Someone carried from a piece of cord a five-foot-tall inflatable pig, dressed in a blue policeman's uniform and holding a club. Navi and a couple of Rent-a-Mobbers huddled around a box of fireworks, to be used as a sort of display once the entire crowd was assembled and Navi had given his speech. These days, to assert your presence in the world, you needed really big signs.

"A lot of the guys want to take over the principal's office," Hedda said, nodding toward those in dog collars. "They want to pull the fire alarm so there'll be police in riot gear here, and we can all get maced and get four column inches and headshots in two leading campus newspapers." She checked her watch and shook her head. Navi lit a bottle rocket, shooting it from a Coke can. We watched it go off, hissing as it was lit, screeching into a brief flight, then making an abrupt nosedive. *"Boys."*

I laughed.

"You're looking really nice," I said.

"Oh, this. I wear this around the squat," she said. "The problem is the other syndicalists don't know how to dress."

"You look really pretty."

"Believe it or not, some guys don't dig fat chicks. I think it's a sign of immaturity."

I was ashamed of myself.

She had a backpack slung across one shoulder.

"Are you hungry?" she said. "I have an apple in here."

"No, thanks."

I didn't see Rose, and I wondered what could be keeping her from this event. Me, probably. The skies were getting darker, the clouds heavier.

More people were assembling onto the field. There were now maybe seventy-five students here, perhaps out of curiosity, wanting to make their stand in the face of authority. I still didn't expect a big crowd.

I heard a boombox playing Urethra Franklin. Somebody among Rent-a-Mob grumbled that they had sold out. Another person, the one carrying the inflatable pig, suggested that Urethra Franklin used ideology as a pose and that they had no integrity to begin with. Take, for instance, Helena St. Pierre, whose image had been appropriated and commercialized. A third person, the one with the boombox, suggested that it was necessary for the movement to have a common identity—in this case, a theme song. He argued that the Balkanized musical tastes of the student population was a divide-and-conquer tactic promoted by the government, which licensed radio stations. And that choice was, in this case, limiting mass unrest. Another person called the third person an RCMP mole. A fifth person suggested the boombox was stolen and was in fact his. A struggle ensued, during which the fifth person smashed the boombox.

"This is no way for anarchists to behave," said Navi, wincing, well aware of the apparent irony.

Hedda told me I looked like my mother.

"People say I take after my old man."

"My parents used to play the St. Pierres in the trailer park. I would prance around in the gravel yard outside in a homemade tutu with 'Bushmills Threnody,' like, blasting away from the kitchen, my dog Sprinkles—the black Lab we had to give away because we could never housebreak him—prancing around with me."

"I'm not a great fan of their music," I said. "But people seem to enjoy it."

She shrugged her shoulders.

"You like what you like. There's not enough pleasure to be fussy."

"Good point."

"I'm all about good points, Saul. When I'm alone in my car, I turn on the oldies station. I was driving up here, and this one station wouldn't stop playing that song because of, *you know*. It was the first time I really listened to your mother's voice as an adult, one who's been in love a few times. I almost drove off the road. I had to turn into the next rest area."

The Indo-Canadian Veterans Legion arrived, about a dozen or so rickety old men who eased out of a blue van parked beside the bleachers, using walkers and canes, wearing crumpled suits and whispery white beards. Navi greeted them, shaking each of their hands. Six months ago, when a Sikh member had been banned from a Veterans Hall, Navi and I organized a petition at our school, and now they were here to support us. The twelve men lined up on the field, each of them taking hold of a giant banner: "Indo-Canadian Veterans Support Human Rights!"

Navi came over to us on the bleachers.

"I don't see any reporters," Navi said to us.

"Whom did you call?" Hedda asked.

"Everyone. They're all at the demo in North Vancouver, taping the quiche."

"Maybe they'll show in a couple of minutes."

"I'm dying out here," Navi said. "Rent-a-Mob is starting to lose interest."

"Is that a reporter?" Hedda asked, pointing to a middle-aged man at the foot of the field, the one I'd seen from my classroom.

"Well, he's not holding a camera."

"He can still be a reporter."

"Rent-a-Mob won't be happy about this."

"Rent-a-Mob's a pack of starfuckers."

"I don't think he looks like a reporter."

"Why?"

"He doesn't look very curious."

For the last three weeks before they left, he read Wallace Stevens aloud to her on a full-size mattress in his attic room in Kitsilano, until the mattress was sold the last week and they slept on the floor. He had a mass of black hair slicked back like one of those reservation boys, she thinks.

After they met outside the Bay, he invited her to a party at his co-op, a stocky Victorian near Jericho Beach. The house had a religious theme: the basement floor, where the bicycles and water heater were found, was painted red, the middle floors green and blue, and the attic room, which one could reach only by stepladder, white. It was a joke among the co-op members, a visual contradiction of the home's faulty heating system, which saw the infernal basement icicle cold much of the year and Nathan the housepainter's joke, seeing that his heavenly room was easily the worst, one with low slanted ceilings and a swampy climate.

That night, in Nathan's room, among his friends, where illicit substances were used, someone picked up a guitar and asked if anyone sang.

Nathan said to Leni, "You must sing, right?"

Later that night, when she first kissed him, she shivered.

Leni Sinclair follows him to Toronto. They take a train across the country, for two days nipping from a tin-silver flask of Jim Beam to take their minds off the Prairies, the stretches of wheat golden in the afternoon sunlight and as wide and deep as the sky above, which was at least five shades of blue, plus fingers of cloud, all of it immobile and massive like a block of marble.

Nathan says both his grandfathers and three great-uncles helped build the railroad.

They nip the whiskey, which they refill from a twenty-six-ounce bottle in the overhead storage, from Sunday to Tuesday, watching the wheat and the telephone poles beside the tracks, joined together by slack black wire and punctuated occasionally by a homely, three-building town, until they reach Ontario, the two of them sighing together in relief, Leni's head against his arm.

Nathan's working on a new look. He has cut his hair and started wearing a clean dress shirt underneath a blue mack jacket. He looks like a Chinese version of those young American men, their backs stiff against their seats, their eyes fixed determinedly on the border guard as they are asked their citizenship and how long they are staying. He's always kept his fingernails clean. He's taking her to meet his uncle, who runs a greasy spoon near the university, specializing in Chinese and Canadian cuisine. "What's Canadian cuisine?" she asks. He shrugs his shoulders.

This is the man your mother loves. Her first love. She puzzles over him. She plays a game. In her mind, she subtracts parts of him: the way he smells, his hands along her back, the sound and quiver of his laugh when her face is clamped to his chest. She tries to locate him among the gestures and words. She subtracts, takes back and dissects until he is faceless, nothing. She does this over and over again, building him back up.

He is sharp and, at times, short-tempered. The week before, he doused her with a glass of lukewarm water during an argument.

Miss you, she thinks, is a tautology.

She is a total sucker.

Nathan Shaw had slender shoulders, a threadbare mustache, narrow eyes and a flat, almost hooked nose. Over his black cardigan, he wore a tan trench coat, his pants cinched up by a black leather belt that sported, for a buckle, something huge and country and western. The expression on his face was of mild indigestion.

I approached him, moving from bleachers to the field. He turned to me, offering a polite smile.

"I didn't know people still did these things."

"Do you want a button?" I asked.

He scratched his chin, his eyebrows lifting thoughtfully.

"It would depend on the button."

I handed him one of Hedda's buttons: two stick figures with their arms raised, "It Takes Two to High-Five" written underneath.

"Thank you," he said, affixing the button to his cardigan. "I thought kids didn't want to change the world anymore. If the world happens to change, young people think, so much the better. But you won't stick your neck out for any such thing. I thought you people were too smart for this."

"That's what my father thinks."

"Nothing new under the sun."

"Are you a parent?"

He shook his head.

"Not to anyone here," he said.

"I thought as much," I said. "You don't look like anyone's parent. Haven't seen you around any open houses."

"I wanted to see what this was all about."

"Have you heard about the book?"

He nodded. His face was wide, and his eyes narrowed when he grinned.

"There are people who want the book banned. You heard about that?" I asked.

"Something about that."

"You heard about the toxic nerve gas."

"Toxic nerve gas is a failure of the imagination. That may

sound old-fashioned, but it's the truth."

"Well, there were threats." I pointed to Navi. "He and I organized the action."

Navi approached us.

"Are you a reporter?" he asked. "Do you need a quote?"

The man in the cardigan shook his head. Navi waved, then ran back into the crowd. He didn't see the resemblance. No one here did, because no one had bothered to read his book, or even glance at its back cover.

"May I ask you a question?"

"Sure," I said.

"Have you read the book?"

"Haven't quite finished it," I said. "Have you?"

He buried his hands into his coat pockets.

"I recognized you from the author's photo."

We watched Navi light another bottle rocket, the explosion followed by a woman shrieking.

"How do you feel, being the cause of all this?" I asked.

"Too old."

I should have asked him why he was here.

"And you came to see this?" I finally asked.

"I happened to be here," said Nathan Shaw, the man for whom my mother had deserted both my father and myself on Labor Day 1980 as he stepped off the field. "I'm in town for something."

"A funeral?" I suggested.

"Nice meeting you."

By the time the accordionist and banjo player arrived, kicking into a low-tempo version of "Mack the Knife," the crowd assembled by Navi, having swelled to maybe half the student population by twelve-thirty, seemed ready to disband right before Navi gave his impassioned denouncement of our school, town, nation and moment in history. Navi introduced me as the person who started the protest earlier this week. This was met with weak applause from Rent-a-Mob.

The walkout succeeded, if only because it had served as a good excuse to leave school early, much like the walkout we had two months ago, an official graduating class of '98 event. A point was made, and now, before things dragged out too long, students were ready to clock out and drive to the beach. The members of Rent-a-Mob seemed a little ornery. They had disappointed, pissy looks on their faces—they had driven forty-five minutes from the city for this.

I didn't have the heart for any of it.

"We're storming the principal's office," Navi said after his speech.

"Have you seen Rose?" I asked.

Navi's eyes narrowed. He looked to the ground, his megaphone dangling from his hand by a leather strap.

So I let Navi go. He and the members of Rent-a-Mob proceeded off the soccer field, their angry signs, their two-piece band playing a vaguely Middle Eastern tune and their inflatable pig in tow. Diapered toddlers and their mothers standing by the chain fences at the very edge of the field, beyond the baseball diamond, watched with interest.

Hedda lagged behind, bent over on the soccer field.

"I have a run in my stocking."

"Sorry."

"Aren't you coming along?"

I shook my head.

"Probably for the best," she said, adjusting her "Miss Police State 1998" sash, which had slipped off when she knelt down.

It started to drizzle as I left school for Rose's. I kept my eyes to my scuffed army boots and the pavement below me, watching drops of rain splatter against the sidewalk, feeling them against my neck. I liked how fresh the air smelled after it rained, and I hoped it would pour. I felt light-headed, the same way I did when I drank coffee on an empty stomach.

I slipped the latch to her backyard and her entrance.

I didn't expect Rose's mother to answer the door. Mrs. Clark was a tall woman whose face was narrow and severe, her hair kept in tight curls. She was in a pair of jeans and a sweatshirt— a change from the lawyer clothes I was used to seeing her in.

"Saul," she said, opening the door just wide enough to crane her head out.

"I'm looking for Rose."

"I'm sorry, Saul," she said. "She's not feeling well. I'm off work looking after her."

"Could I see her for a minute?"

"I don't think this is a good time." Mrs. Clark eyed me sharply, and I wondered how much Rose had told her about us. "Sorry," she added softly. She never especially liked me. I was the one Rose spent nights with when she was supposed to be making good grades. I wondered whether she would have been so polite if she hadn't known about my mother. For a moment I was glad to be so pitiable.

"I'm sorry, Saul," she repeated, this time as if to say I should go. I heard a toilet flush and the washroom door opening from

Rose's room. Mrs. Clark began to close the door. "If you want, I could give her a message."

"Tell her I said hello."

Mrs. Clark nodded and closed the door.

It never really did rain. By early evening, most of the clouds had parted, leaving the sky smeared in bronze.

Jana was over at Dale's. Rather than be alone, I returned to my father's house. The kitchen still sat half finished, so we took dinner outside again. Dad had ordered Chinese food from a pretty decent place in town and the dishes came hot in round, aluminum containers. I sat in a lawn chair beside Marina, who had on her aviator sunglasses again and wore two silver butterfly barrettes in her hair, as she drank margaritas. Louise came out with a stack of dishes.

"I think they packed disposable chopsticks along with the food," I said.

Louise placed a blue-checkered cloth on the table and then peeled off the lid from one dish. Steam rose from the beef and broccoli.

"Gord and Nadine said they might come by, though they might be late," she said. She held the shiny tin lid up so that it reflected in the sun.

"Nadine's just come out of the hospital for food poisoning," Marina said. "Maybe she won't be too hungry."

Louise snorted and fit the lid back on the dish.

"Douche bag," she said, as she went back into the house through the sliding door.

"What's up with her?"

"She's upset with me," Marina said. "She thinks I'm stealing

your father again. I was out of the shower, and my towel just sort
of fell off. A guy gives you a look, and suddenly *you're the whore*."

"You don't want to give someone the wrong idea."

"Men all think the same," she said. Marina was wearing a blue
cashmere sweater and a matching skirt with a slit up her right
thigh. I felt my throat tighten, my hands balling in jealousy. "Just
kidding." She smiled, teeth on bottom lip, and squeezed my
knee. "I was just trying to get your attention. I wanted to make
you jealous."

Marina giggled, her laugh stinging and mocking like a dozen
tiny paper cuts. She lit a cigarette, her head falling back against
her shoulders as she exhaled. The green nail polish on her
short fingernails was chipped and worn away.

Dad, Richard and Andreas came outside carrying liter-sized
beer steins. Richard and Andreas were both wearing trucker
shirts that they must have borrowed from my father. Dad was
in khaki shorts, his hair greased back and ponytailed. He
seemed surprised to see me.

"Saul," he said, double-taking in feigned astonishment.
"You've been here an awful lot."

I wanted to hit him very hard.

"I understand your stepmother's remarrying." He sounded as
matter-of-fact as he could. But his mouth tightened, and there
was something twitchy in his eyes. I nodded. "Gord spoke to
her. How is she?"

"She's happy," I said. I waited for Dad to say more, looking
as if he wanted to. Instead he mentioned seeing the walkout at
school on TV.

"It brought back memories," Dad said, chuckling, his face
pink. "Those were glory days." He sat down at the picnic table

with Andreas, drinking from his giant mug of beer. "And you organized that? Remarkable. I always suspected I was raising a radical."

"We were protesting the censorship of a book."

"How very noble of you. And the world thanks you."

"I think a healthy participation in political activism is necessary in the life of a student," Louise said, opening a container of hot-and-sour soup.

"The book is called *Baroque-a-Nova*, by Nathan Shaw," I said, in the hope Dad would holler or curse, anything.

My father wasn't terribly tall and the way he walked, back all hunched up, made him look shorter. Dad squinted his silvery eyes and wrinkled his forehead, as if he were trying to figure a riddle or a punch line. He coughed.

"Well," he said, "the future is in good hands. Next I suppose you'll be picketing me for crimes against humanity or whatever."

"Do you know," Louise said brightly, "that there's a large man who wants to rape and shoot Ian?"

"A very large man," I corrected.

Dad shook his head. "Those looney tunes think I've done everything to your mother, women and native people in general."

"Did you see that quiche on TV?" Louise asked. "Did you see it? It was so big. The police pulled the protestors off the bridge, so all there was was that big quiche. It was huge, like forty-eight feet in diameter. It was like an aboveground swimming pool. How much leek would you need for something that big? I mean, you don't have to use leek, but it's for the best—trust me."

Dad was drunk, and once again he was staring at Marina,

who was trying to avoid eye contact. A loose, indecent smile spread across his face.

"Well, hello, my pretty," he drawled.

Richard picked up a lawn chair leaning against the picnic table and unfolded it beside me.

"Nice duds," Marina said.

"What is the meaning of this idiomatic expression, this 'duds'?"

"We've been conducting, shall we say, a language exchange," Marina said, turning to me, a gleeful expression on her face. "Listen to this: *Deine Oma hat Hängetitten!*"

Richard started snorting like a schoolboy. "Ha, ha. You just said, 'Your grandmother has sagging breasts.'"

"*Mein Leben ist nur ein Haufen Kacke!*"

"'My life is a pile of crap.'"

"*Sie verkaufen viel Scheissdreck an die Turisten!*"

"'They sell a lot of shitty junk to the tourists.'"

Marina pointed to his lumberjack shirt.

"Duds."

"Duds," he repeated. "Yeah, is very radical, right?" he said, admiring his shirt. We nodded. "I am feeling, like, comfortable in this country. I believe the Canadian soul is to be found in absence and distance, in its native traditions."

"You mean like totem poles?" Marina said. "I suppose we are in the Pacific Northwest. Or do Canadians call this area the southwest?"

I gave her a dirty look.

"I want to ask you, Saul," Richard said, touching my hand, "about your native heritage, your mother. Quickly, because I do not have very much time. I have finished speaking to your father and this friend, the pedal-steel player, this Gordon. Now, before I return to Germany, I must speak to you. Tomorrow is good, yeah?"

"I don't think so." There was my mother's involuntary valediction, and of course my father's idiotic rebuttal. My father, who said nothing to me, nothing to Jana, practically spewing his life when a camera was turned on him.

"Then Sunday," Richard said. "Urethra Franklin leaves for Japan on Sunday, and I must follow shortly thereafter."

"I'd rather not."

"Do I frighten you?" he said. His voice rose, sharp and high, and the beer in his hand trembled. "Does my accent bewilder you? Do you find my manner brusque and iconoclastic?"

"Excuse me?"

"Why do you insist on jeopardizing my career? Why do you resist me?"

"Richard, can you lay off?" Marina said. "Saul is telling you he's no media whore."

Dad grunted.

Richard took a sip from his beer, then wiped a line of foam from his upper lip. He stood up from his lawn chair and placed his hand on my father's back. Dad's flannel shirt was a little too small for him around the shoulders, but he still looked better in it than my father.

"Please, Ian, talk to your son."

"Richard," Dad said, "all I ever do is talk."

The arrangements had been made. The body of my mother was expected to arrive on Saturday. There was to be a viewing Sunday, a Catholic funeral and burial Monday. The speeches would be given Sunday, since Catholic services were more formal—long-winded and impersonal, Dad said, little more than regular Masses with coffins. Already, I was told, there were people in town from Toronto and New York and San Francisco, touring band members, backup singers and record people from the days of the St. Pierres—friends of my parents whom my father had lost touch with in the eighteen years since my mother's disappearance. And more to come. People who came to mourn a woman who thought so much of them that she vanished to another continent.

Gord and Nadine arrived. Gord passed by me, clapping a hand on my shoulder. He was wearing an old pair of denim flares and a Captain Beefheart T-shirt. He smiled and pulled me into a headlock. I tensed up in his grip and he let me go. He asked how I was doing and I nodded senselessly.

Nadine looked pale in a pair of white cutoffs and a pink sleeveless shirt, her hair tied into two pigtails. She was still wearing her hospital bracelet.

"How are you feeling?" Marina asked, nibbling on a piece of honey-and-garlic sparerib.

"Terrible," Nadine said. "Simply miserable."

"It was only a little food poisoning," Gord said.

"Says you," Nadine said. She was looking at her fingernails. "One of the doctors was about this close to amputating a leg."

"That never happened, Nadine."

"I was at death's door."

"Not true."

"You have no clue. I don't think you even tried to understand how I felt lying in the hospital all alone."

"Alone? I was with you the whole time."

"I was alone, *Gord*—metaphorically—because no one knew how I felt."

"Sometimes I don't understand a word you're saying."

"They said I was this close to needing a liver transplant."

Dad came back from the house with his old reel-to-reel tape player. He put the machine on the picnic table and spooled a tape with "Labor Day 1980" marked on it, just as he promised Richard. We listened to my mother's recorded voice here, in my father's backyard, for the second time this week. There was applause and then the opening chords to "Great Slave Lake," the first song on the St. Pierres' fifth and final album, *Broken Heart's Daydream*:

> I want to ask you something before you wake
> I've been thinking how the summer must end
> Will our love fade like the sun against Great Slave Lake?
> Will our love fade like the sun against Great Slave Lake?
>
> At the farm I trace the days you're in the city
> Against the dew on the windowpanes
> Will our love fade like the sun against Great Slave Lake?
> Will our love fade like the sun against Great Slave Lake?
>
> I feel like I'm losing time
> Mired in the crickets' chime
> Until I feel your breath against my cheek
> Let us sleep in an embrace
> Let me dream of your sweet face
> How wonderful to make true
> This song of love I sing to you

Our love will rise again
Like the sun against Great Slave Lake
Our love will rise again
Like the sun against Great Slave Lake

"Yeah, this suicide made everything so very disorganized. When we arrived in Bangkok, we tried ringing her," Richard said, "but she didn't pick up her phone. She lived in Potpang." Richard shook his head. "Not a nice area. We asked Helena's neighbors in the housing complex about her, but they knew nothing of this red-skinned woman—only that she was polite and kind, but remained alone. We tried to find her church where she did her missionary work, but a taxi driver took us to a Pizza Hut and brandished a knife in our faces when we protested. We decided to knock at her door. We didn't expect her to react in such a way when we found her, that she would be so, so *unreasonable*."

"And you expected, what?" I asked.

"What happened was lamentable," Richard said, sounding defensive and irritated, "but I acted as would a journalist."

"Do you think she moved to Thailand because she wanted you to find her?"

Richard said nothing.

Dad scratched the back of his neck, his eyes soft and far away, apparently lost in the music.

"Christ," Louise said, "I was seven when this recording was made. I'm surprised the tape sounds as good as it does."

Marina stood by the reel-to-reel.

"I think seventies stereo technology is cooler," she said. "It was the age of beanbags and lava lamps, when stereos were meant to be in the basement. These days you get stereos in little components, and the stereos are black or gray. They're so boring. The designs were sleeker back then. The knobs were bigger."

"Slut," Louise said.

The next few songs were from *Bushmills Threnody*, the album, not the song, and the second album, *Winnipeg Snowfall*. Then the later stuff. The applause heard was noticeably less enthusiastic for all the songs from the last two albums. They sold poorly, in spite of my father's best efforts to give listeners what they wanted.

When she performed, my mother would utter not a single word to the audience. From all accounts, she stood there completely still, a small, thin woman with eyes like dark thoughts. She was impervious to their applause, the howls and wolf whistles, the song requests. The flashbulbs would reflect off her as she waited blank-faced for it to die down. That was before she started hearing things.

Gord smiled, his horsy, gummy mouth open wide, and tapped his foot along to the music.

Nadine found nail clippers in her purse and started clipping her toenails at the picnic table.

Richard and Andreas held their liter-sized beer steins against their chests, their heads dropped solemnly.

Louise sat next to Dad, her mouth in a hard, unforgiving frown, glaring at Marina.

Marina was down in the lawn chair beside me. She seemed upset, her arms crossed, her eyes clear and empty, her mouth twiching indignantly.

The early evening sun fell upon us, warm, forgiving, absent-minded.

We heard the sound of a sprinkler in the yard next to us, whisking in the air, water splattering.

The air smelled like mown grass.

I pitied my father. I sat in my lawn chair with my ankles crossed underneath, all my blood, it would seem, rushing to my ears. He didn't say anything. He drank his beer and listened to the cracks and breaths of my mother's voice, to the Moog synthesizer's transistor-driven keening, to Gord's pedal steel sweetly gliding toward a major seven chord, to his own chiming twelve-string. Dad let out a little groan after each song, every song leading closer to the show's end. I wondered where he thought he was right now, whether he wasn't in his mind locating himself on that stage. I would have let my memory fail.

"What's your problem?" Marina asked from her lawn chair after the recording had ended. Dad was inside, returning the tape to his closet.

"Your little slutty ass," Louise said, stacking the dishes.

"Bite me."

"At least I'm not named after a place where they store boats."

"Cunt."

"Home away from home for wayward sailors."

"Fuckface."

"The last stop for solitary seamen, sinking their anchors."

"A fifty-year-old man wanting to fuck you doesn't mean more than it does. It just is what it is."

"I think you're jealous," Louise said.

"Why would I be jealous of you? What do you have that I'd want?"

"A father. A trust fund. A happy childhood."

Marina said nothing, her eyes still, looking away past the back fence to the highway. Louise arranged the dishes in a pile and picked them up, as if to leave for the kitchen. Then she put them back on the table.

"You need male attention so badly that you'll fuck anyone between the ages of fifty and eighteen," Louise said.

The whole lot of us sat there silently until Dad came back out, wearing a pair of sunglasses.

"The funeral's Monday, folks," he said. He turned to Louise. "What's your damage?"

Louise, her hand covering her mouth, disappeared into the kitchen with the dishes. We heard the faucet running.

"I try to tell her to stop," Dad said, nodding toward ever-helpful Louise, "but the girl can't help herself."

Marina rolled down the window and rested her arm against the door. Even now, after the sun had set, the air and the pavement still felt warm. The streetlights along Trunk Road buzzed prematurely, pale white in the orange twilight sky, as the days had grown longer and more reluctant to give way to darkness.

"I can understand why you want to get out of here," Marina said quietly.

"How do you know I want to leave?"

"Who would want to stay?" she asked impatiently. "What are you waiting for?"

Maybe she had been trying to hit on my father. Maybe she was hurt and fucked up, and she acted in certain ways to get the attention of men. I was willing to overlook that. I wanted her that badly.

We turned onto the highway at Trunk Road and moved southbound.

"Where are you taking me?"

We drove through Tsawwassen, past the ferries that led to Vancouver Island, turning into a side road flanked by cow pastures and tulip fields and cherry trees until we reached a small public beach, just off from a new condominium development. We parked in the empty lot, on a dune overlooking the beach and the ocean. I cut the engine. I could hear myself breathing.

"This is where you take your girlfriend?" she asked.

I nodded.

She looked at me, a stern expression on her face. Then she moved toward me, holding my stare. I dropped my hand against her hip and ran it up, against soft flesh and rib bone, up until I felt her bra. I tried not to burp when I kissed her; we ended up banging teeth instead. I tasted the cigarette smoke on her breath with my eyes half open. The corners of her mouth lifted into a smile and then fell. I kissed her again—slowly, wetly and well.

"I think," she said, "everyone deserves a second chance."

"Thank you," I said. "Thank you very much."

I sat there, my chest hollowing, feeling good about the world. Every moment should be like this—one that could be relived, rehearsed and consumed over and over again, prepared for and wanly imagined.

"Do you like my barrettes?" she asked, pointing to the shiny butterflies in her hair.

I nodded. I thought she said something else.

She laughed.

I sat there thinking I should quit now. We moved to the back, climbing over the emergency brake, and undressed underneath a blanket my dad kept folded above the passenger seat beside the first-aid kit and the rear stereo speakers. I felt Marina's tongue flicking between my teeth, her short fingernails, the cracked green nail polish on them, along my back. I felt her stomach. I was hard and Marina straddled me between her legs and I could smell the sea on her skin.

Saturday

We were on our way to the funeral home on the far side of town, the windshield wipers of Dad's car squeaking as they swept off the rain, which fell in fine pellets. He let me tag along, Louise in the passenger side, me in the back where I ended up with Marina last night. I didn't know why Louise bothered to come, why she needed to drape herself around my father at this time. Not that there was an especially good time for any of this. Dad was dressing better, even respectably. Maybe he felt the clothes suited the occasion, or maybe he was hoping to impress. All this week he had shaved regularly, worn clean shirts tucked into dark corduroys and jeans. Yet the effort and preening didn't suit his threadbare soul. He looked sad.

"So I read this book by this Nathan Shaw guy, the one that was banned at Saul's school," Louise said. "I've been meaning to read it for a while. It was nominated for an award back in the seventies, an award given by an island, one of those Island Council Association–something awards that make you think of pregnant women in flares and kerchiefs." She lowered her voice: "It's about her, isn't it, Ian? It's about Helena."

Dad shrugged his shoulders. He mumbled, "She was supposed to have left with him. A fling. That's what I understood."

"Not that it's a bad book. It's all right; it's a quick read. A first novel by any definition. Okay, sometimes Mr. Shaw goes off on tangents, but he has a lot of metaphors for crying—like thirty or forty of them. I really can't say it's worth public outcry—you know, toxic nerve gas threats. The public does what it sees fit."

"Just like fickle women."

Louise kept running her mouth. She was nervous because Dad and I weren't saying much. She mentioned her screenplay. She suggested Dad take a vacation after the funeral, glancing at Ian for a reaction and then out the window, her tiny head ping-ponging back and forth. My dad looked straight ahead silently, neither menacing nor malicious, as when he seethed, when he'd plotted against Jana and me at the dinner table, yelling at Jana for spending, at me for general turpitude. Today he lacked conviction. He looked the way he did sitting alone in the kitchen strumming a guitar, rhyming words to G chords quietly, a pen and notepad on the table, before losing it, knowing there would be no one to sing whatever he wrote in any event, putting his guitar carefully back into its case, replacing it on the top shelf of his closet.

Dad looking slightly pissed off, knuckles taut on the steering wheel, staring ahead with a hollowed-out expression, cross-eyed in grief.

We pulled into the Silver and Gold Motor Inn. A man wearing a priest's collar stood in the parking lot, stepping over a puddle to get to us.

"Ian St. Pierre?" he asked. He carried his height awkwardly, had a long neck and hips that widened below his waist, like a woman.

"Father Felix?"

They shook hands. Felix got into the seat next to me.

"Father Felix," Dad explained, "worked with Leni in Thailand. The two of them helped the poor."

"She was a kind woman," he said. "She was at the parish before me—showed me the ropes, really. I was new."

"I spoke to Felix after your mother died," Dad said. "He was so kind to deal with the people at the embassy and escort the body home."

"I suggested it. Didn't want to miss her funeral. If there was anything I could do, could've done, you know."

Felix's eyes fell on me, small blue gumdrops on his saucer-of-milk face—a twenty-year-old face, not a day older. He wore his hair swept sideways, with liberal amounts of hairspray so it held solid and unnaturally, as if he were wearing an ugly wig. His chubby neck chafed in his collar.

Louise smiled at Father Felix. "May I ask you a question?"

"You were wondering about my age?"

"I'm sorry," she said. "I meant to be subtle."

"Oh, no. I get it all the time. I started young and I look younger, but I've been with the Church almost ten years." He chuckled. "It puts off some people at first, so I go out of my way to explain. I received the call when I was eighteen."

"That sounds pretty eager."

Father Felix considered this, then laughed politely.

"I'd imagine eighteen-year-olds would have other things on their minds besides God," Louise said.

"I guess. But I wasn't too different. I lusted," he said, chuckling nervously in recollection. "Then I received the call."

Louise looked amused.

"What was that like? Did you hear the voice of God?"

"No, not exactly. The Virgin Mary appeared at the foot of my bed when I was in my senior year of high school. It was a shocking experience, something I was completely unprepared for. Before then, you couldn't say I was terribly concerned about religion."

"You had a religious epiphany. Just like Helena St. Pierre." Louise said this a little sourly, with a hint of mockery that Felix chose to ignore.

"She was a sweet woman."

"Mary or Helena St. Pierre?"

"Both."

We drove past a senior watering his lawn amidst ceramic lawn ornaments and a miniature windmill. A wire fence separated the cemetery from the rest of the neighborhood. Pink and gray marble headstones dotted one side of a patchy lawn, the other side reserved for nameplates. The bouquets and arrangements on both were matted down by the rain.

The parking lot covered the area between a mausoleum, a stone building with stained French windows, framed by hedges, and the funeral home office. We parked next to a white pickup truck with a small orange crane in its cab and went along a tiled path through a garden, past a pond and two park benches, a bronze plaque on the lawn reading "Restrooms," with an arrow

pointing to the office and chapel, a whitewashed complex comprising two steep blacktopped roofs. Once inside the chapel, we
went down a long hallway lined with octagonal windows. At
every window was a table with a floral arrangement and a box of
Kleenex. At the end of the hall was the office, which was soft
and carpeted like a doctor's office, only with more Kleenex. The
receptionist behind the counter asked us to sit, then picked up
a phone. She was a trim woman in her thirties, wearing a summer blouse and sandals. She put down the phone and said
someone would be talking to us shortly. I sat in a stiff leather
armchair next to a water cooler, flipping through the *Times* and
*Entertainment Weekly*s fanned across a glass-topped coffee table,
opposite a portrait of a serious-looking man in a blue suit. Dad
stood, his hands in his slacks, pacing in a circle.

A man in a dark suit appeared. He had a narrow face, a hair-
line that dropped far back and a bushy, graying mustache. He
shook our hands with a firm, clammy grip. He looked like a
direct descendant of the man in the portrait. "I'm Mr. Dirk," he
said. "Follow me." He led us down another hall until we
reached the room where the viewing would be held, the
chapel. We entered from the rear entrance, through a dimly lit
reception area with low-slung chairs and a long table next to
two heavy doors. It was a cream-colored room, not so big, the
pews backed with maroon cushions. Stale light fell through the
skylights in the peaked, maple ceiling. There was a lectern up
front. Next to it, the wheels of a coffin had left grooves in the
salmon-pink plush carpeting. The room smelled like cedar oil.

Louise tugged Dad's denim shirtsleeve.

"This is where the funeral's being conducted?" Louise asked.

"Just the viewing," Dad said, mumbling. He looked distracted, hunched over, as if he were counting with his hands in his pockets. "The funeral's Monday, at a church."

"We understand this might be an unusual case," the man in the suit said. "We've been taking calls from the press ourselves—discreetly, of course." My father nodded. "Should we discuss the schedule of the viewing and burial here or in my office?"

"Of course," Dad said. Then, after a timid gulp, "Once I see her body."

"Perhaps we might address more immediate concerns. There is, for instance, the issue of the music to be played. Our organist is very talented—he also used to do weddings and arena sporting events before they took to using tapes. There are the flower arrangements and method of payment, as well."

Dad persisted. The smile on the funeral director's face seemed to peel away, his voice trailing off. The body was not yet prepared for viewing, he explained.

"I think it would be better for me if I saw her," he said.

"It's been almost twenty years," I said. "Can't you wait?"

Dad ignored me. It was blood lust, I thought.

"Honestly," Mr. Dirk said finally, his voice sharper, "she's a mess." Dad kept his eyes on the funeral director until, with a tired smirk, he relented. They disappeared through a side exit.

Father Felix stood by a pew, inspecting the cushions.

"I was just thinking," Felix said to me, a big smile on his face, "how you must be the very same age I was when I joined the Church."

"Oh," I said, nodding politely. I pictured myself in black, saying prayers and giving communion, and felt nervous as hell.

"Enjoy yourself now, Saul. You'll regret it otherwise." He

sighed wistfully. "It was certainly a difficult time in my life. I had trouble keeping my mind on things."

"Hormones."

"I remember my first vision of Mary. She was in a halter top and fishnets. A fine-looking young woman. Very healthy. Robust."

Louise was standing at the podium in a flower-print blouse and shorts, leaning against it. There were padded benches at either side behind the podium, and flags.

"What do you do in Thailand, Father Felix?" she asked.

"We run a home for the kids—young women, mostly. There are a lot of orphans in Bangkok. There's a choir."

"And were you close to Helena?"

Felix's face went red. He struggled to get out a word.

"I was shy around her, I must admit," he said with hesitation. "I suppose I'm generally a shy person. I admired her. We did some work together in the country, where they don't treat children well, especially young girls."

"They sell their daughters," Louise said.

Father Felix sighed. "I'm afraid they do."

I stared up at the overcast sky, brown and impenetrable, through the skylights. This whole place was creepy.

Last night, I had dreamt about my mother for the first time since the suicide. I saw her in my father's backyard sliding open the glass door, Dad beside the grill in an apron, wiping his brow with the inside of his forearm, Marina and Louise, Jana and Rose at the picnic table. She sat down and ate with us. We were surprised to see her, but no one said a word to her. We just watched her eating and eating. All she did in my dream was eat. I forgot what happened next. I didn't remember what she looked like in my dream, or if I even said anything to her. I woke up and there was a moment before I realized I had been dreaming, my heart filling that instant before it returned to normal.

In another room, I imagined my mother's body lying on a slab of stainless steel, wrapped in plastic.

"Your father's been very generous. He paid my way here, provided for my lodging. You must thank him again for me."

"Sure." And I wondered how my father suddenly became so generous. He usually had his reasons. To impress, to appease, to apologize. I felt a shudder run down my neck and ripple through my spine to my knees.

"Are you a friend of Saul's?" he asked Louise.

"I'm a friend of Ian's," she said, looking at me from the corners of her eyes. Her mouth closed, tight and small.

Felix nodded, as if to say he understood.

I sat down, resting my head against the row ahead of me.

"You look like you're praying," Louise said.

I started banging my head against the pew.

"Did she speak about me?"

Father Felix rubbed the corners of his eyes with his thumb and forefinger as though he had allergies or was groggy. "Saul, she was very troubled."

"What was my mother like, Father Felix?" I asked.

She was in another room, a corpse.

It is one dramatic exit after another, a departure appropriate for someone who actively seeks excitement, a woman who has forsaken her clothes for an Introduction to Life Etching, in public, in front of photographers, paper and charcoal extra, a black-eyed waif hard-wired for impulsiveness. That's why she beats the men off with a stick, even putting your dad into fits of chain-smoking sullenness, his neck hunched, a frown on his wretched face. As much as he philanders and bosses and cajoles her, he is whipped. For whatever hurt he doles out to her, enough pain to force her away from the world, she returns tenfold in her silence. She is moody and terrified to step on the stage, quickly slighted and spiteful in her small-boned way. Fame aggravates every one of her tics. It makes her more alluring, more solitary, more pitiful, more difficult, more easily bored. In her voice, she bestows on the music, the vapid mushy folk, its shadows, its low-riding heart.

Say your mother's been hearing things, like a radio crossed between two stations, the steel twang of a blues weeper cutting into the knuckled vowels of three Scotsmen debating federalism on the AM band. The drugs were making her fat, so she stopped using them, and then they returned, louder and even more urgent, like a busload of children stalled in the snow.

Once she lets go, she finds herself relieved. She sits in the dark and listens to her brain humming. She sleeps with them talking to her.

She doesn't intend to sing the encore. Instead, she speeds past security people and the opening band watching *That's Incredible* and drinking white wine that smells like nail-polish remover, through basement corridors, her cowboy boots clacking down a fire escape and out into the summer night. They wait for her onstage for ten minutes, the audience responding with heavier applause, stamping their feet on the dance floor, which is springy because of the old rubber tires crammed underneath. Dad runs backstage and yells at everyone. An assistant sent to her dressing room comes back with no Leni. Dad rolls his eyes and proceeds to inform everyone present that their value has plummeted below their weight in pigeon shit.

The band plays an unrehearsed version of "Peter Gunn," with an extended drum break, to kill time. The crowd sounds pissy. Someone throws a quarter at the band, welting Gord on the forehead—the punk culture, the yobs dragging us into the sewer once and for all, in the process making music like the St. Pierres' sound overproduced and glossy, a landing zone for derision.

The stage is as dark as a witch's cauldron, the room stewing with humidity, swelling with idle sweat. A single spotlight rests on a microphone in the middle of the proscenium. Dad turns to Jana in her dashiki, her hands folded over her chest. "You know where she is, don't you?" he asks. "Tell me," he screams. Jana, who is by then secretly, desperately in love with him, denies everything.

Say your mother wants less of this world. Say she wants it to collapse into her pocket. She wants less of her husband, his clinging and abuse, his schedules and bitter words. It would be impossible to stop the tour, for them to divorce and skulk out of courtrooms with their collars turned up, for child custody to be established, bank accounts located and sorted and halved. In spite of her protests, he has carried on as if they had no choice about the tour, the radio-station interviews and auto-graph sessions, that they are simply unable to walk away from it all. So she calls an old boyfriend—the dependable one who never forgot her in his heart—to pick her up, mid-tour, to run off with her and drive his rental car to the airport. Eventually she'll cut him loose, too.

Ian steps onto the stage on Labor Day 1980, toward the spot-light to make an announcement. The crowd cackles, expecting

Helena St. Pierre. He turns back without saying a word and tells
the stage manager to turn on the lights—show's over.

I watched Father Felix in the chapel, a wedge of light falling
like a hand onto his shoulder as he stood underneath a skylight.
He started to answer my question when Dad returned from the
same side entrance from which he'd left. He looked pale, his
face sour with grief. Mr. Dirk extended a handkerchief to him,
pressed and silk, as red as a valentine. Dad took it. Louise
started to say something, but Dad waved her off with his borrowed hanky. He told her to shut up. Dad wiped a thin white
string of puke from his chin, then sat next to me, his head rocking back and forth, mouth open, my forehead pressed against
the pew, exhausted, conscious, the two of us, father and son.

A large woman in a dull brown apron stood behind the counter
of the doughnut shop in front of the glazes and almond pow-
ders and pink sprinkles being offered. She looked familiar and
smiled at me as I walked in. She had a small upturned nose and
was fat, her hands ashen in clear plastic gloves, holding a pair
of kitchen tongs.

"How are you?" she asked.

"I'm fine."

"And how is your stepmother?"

"Jana's fine."

"And how is your father?"

"My father's fine."

"Your father should be shot like the dog he is."

The doughnut shop was in the strip mall, with its flat and
khaki stucco exteriors and its shopping carts neatly slotted

together beside shrubbed traffic islands, three blocks off the gentrified main drag. This was the unpopular strip mall—the one with the thrift store and fabric warehouse. Across the street was a newer development with two coffeehouses and a shop devoted to fancy soaps. The new mall bought into a West Coast lifestyle talked about in magazines, where people my parents' age, who ended up as lawyers and computer executives and therapists, took tai chi classes and purchased Mexican hand-blown glass. My parents were among the few people of their generation who chose not to settle down and become respectable. They were failures.

Marina was waiting for me at the table by the window, stirring her coffee with a red plastic stick. In front of her on her tray, sitting on a square piece of wax paper, were glazed chocolate doughnut holes.

Two white men in flannel shirts and steel-toed boots sat in the booth next to us, reading their sports pages and eyeing Marina, sneering at me for whatever reason—who knows. On account that I was a skinny, ethnic boy with greasy hair, in my Nomeansno T-shirt and my combat pants, not quite out of high school, from a broken home. There was craziness in my family, from both sides. It ran through my veins like the cars speeding along the highway at night. Craziness and hormones. A Muzak version of a Clash song was playing in the shop, Marina, not really thinking, tapping a fingernail, newly painted in silver sparkle, against the yellow tabletop to the beat. I felt sort of nervous and sort of bad, a little cocky because I could still taste her skin, mostly anxious because the taste grew faint.

I popped a doughnut hole in my mouth, wiping glaze from the corner of my mouth with my shirtsleeve.

"What is your fascination with doughnuts?" she asked.

"The typical fascination."

She laughed again.

Her mouth tight and pursed as she drank her creamed coffee, her teeth resting on her bottom lip as she smiled, her lips a brick, earthy red—the color of a dried wound.

I felt like crying. "Rose likes doughnut holes, too."

"Oh," Marina said. "How is your girlfriend?"

"She hasn't been returning my calls."

Doughnuts were among the first things Rose would swear off when she decided to lose weight. Rose would diet and swim two hours a day, but her metabolism was awful and she just wouldn't get any thinner. I hated seeing her diet. I pictured her at school eating her whole-wheat and alfalfa sandwiches. It made me feel like crying.

Marina rested her chin against the heel of her hand and took a sip of her coffee. She tucked a strand of hair behind her ears, her mouth set in a pained expression, slightly quivering.

"My mom's a psychic, you know that?"

I shook my head.

"A one-nine-hundred-number type who works out of her house, at her kitchen table. She spends her evenings drinking Tom Collinses with dates she meets through newspaper ads and services. She says it's the easiest way to meet nice men. One night when I was twelve, after my stepfather had run out, my mother put pictures of three men on the kitchen table. 'I have it narrowed down to these three,' she told me. 'You decide.'"

"Last night," I felt compelled to say, "was my fault."

She blushed. "You're sweet," she said, laughing, "to take the blame."

Marina in pigtails, wearing her pearl earrings and stringy rubber bracelets, in a blue tank top and matching skirt. She nodded and made a violin bowing motion in the air. I didn't know exactly what she meant by that, whether she was making fun of me or sympathizing. There lay the attraction.

She finished her coffee and suggested we leave.

"Your father should be shot like the dog he is," the woman behind the counter said.

She looked familiar, though I couldn't exactly locate her, with her chubby fingers and her highlighted, sandy brown hair. She was stupid looking, like Nadine almost, stupid and loud and opinionated. She must have been a fan.

"Who are you?" I asked. Marina hung by my side, looking ready to go.

"You don't remember me?"

I said I didn't.

"I haven't seen you in years, since you were a tiny infant. But all this time I've been watching you."

We heard some banging outside. There was Anders rapping against the plate-glass window, holding a bouquet of white daisies, all the brighter against his dusky face.

"I called the school. They won't teach his filthy book any-more."

"Not you again," the doughnut lady said, leaving her spot at the corner. Was she his hard, hard woman? She seemed peculiar enough. "I told you to buzz off."

"The lies they tell about you," Anders yelled.

"Go," she said as she went to the door. "I have work to do."

The corners of Anders's mouth turned back. He sprinted away, dropping his daisies as he ran. She squatted down to pick up the little white flowers and threw them in a trash can inside. Out in the parking lot, kids on mountain bikes, ten-year-olds in dusty baseball uniforms, whipped by us from the convenience store, with one hand on their bikes and orange and purple Mr. Freezes in the other.

Marina and I went to the thrift store occupying the space that was once a supermarket. The windows took up its face, and the high ceilings sloped up at the middle. Crockery and appliances—once-white blenders and dented toaster ovens, their windows filmy from grease fires—were off to the side, as we entered next to shelves of used Harlequins, their spines cracked white, menswear and womenswear to the left, shoes and children's clothes at the back. A young Indian woman was working the only register open, ringing in a pair of plat-form shoes for a purple-haired girl, who held a skateboard at her hip.

I watched Marina flipping through outfits, the wire coat hangers and their plastic clips clicking against one another as she did. When she found something promising, she folded it over her forearm.

She looked up at me and smiled.

"I didn't expect to be here this long. I pack lightly."

The dressing-room doors were like those of a saloon in a Western. I waited outside as Marina changed, holding on to her coat hangers. I could see her bare shoulders and her skirt falling to her ankles and bunching on the floor.

She appeared in a black suit jacket with shoulder pads and a white polka-dot collar.

"Too sexy," she said.

She came out in two other dark dresses before I realized that she was dressing for a funeral.

"Sometimes I think my breasts are a fucking curse," she said. She cupped them in her hands and studied them, a pleasantly surprised look on her face. "I take that back."

I watched Marina undress again later that afternoon, though this time in my old room. She unbuttoned her skirt and folded it on a chair, over which she placed her bra, black, undone at the front.

We heard the front door open and close, then the floor-boards creaking, the sound of someone making their way to the kitchen.

I sat on the cot. The curtains had yet to be drawn. I could see the neighbors' yard over her shoulder. They never turned off their sprinkler in the summer. They were terrible, terrible people, I decided.

We heard Louise asking if anyone was home.

Marina stood in front of me, her body lined in daylight.

It wasn't illegal, what we were doing. I was eighteen years old and consenting—in a big way. And these were the suburbs, after all. She moved two steps toward me demurely, a little smile on her face, her eyes bright like she was thinking about a joke she'd just heard, the one Freud told comparing marriage to an umbrella—sooner or later you take a cab. She stood before me, her knees scraping against mine, allowing me to inspect her, to admire her. I examined her for imperfections, scrupu-lously like a jeweler, handling her with the tips of my thumb and forefinger. I looked for scars, purple blotches on an inner thigh, pale white lines from surgery, butterfly-shaped moles. I didn't find any.

I told her I loved her.

She shook her head.

I traced a fingernail from above her pussy, up her waist to the bone between her breasts. She took my cock with her thumb and index finger and gave it a couple of tugs, a frisky look on her face.

"Lie down," I said.

"The magic word is what."

"What." I paused. "Please."

She smiled and sat down at the edge of the narrow bed. I leaned into her, her breath against my neck, and we were horizontal. She swung her feet onto the bed, her knees slightly raised.

I slipped down until I was between her legs, my hands on her hips. I kissed her stomach and her inner thighs. I ran my tongue along the outer lips of her pussy, then split them open with my fingers, moved my tongue up and down until I found her clitoris. Her legs shuddered. I stopped.

"I haven't done this before."

"Take your time," she said, in a whisper. She giggled, tickled. "Start slow, regularly, then, um, you know, pick up the pace."

We found Louise in the living room, smoking cloves and typing away at her laptop. Two airplane-sized bottles of rum sat on the coffee table, one empty. She raised a hand at us, with almost regal disinterest, but continued typing. Once she finished whatever she was typing, she looked up, surprised to see us.

"Oh, there you are," she said. "Did you just get in?"

"Where's Ian?" Marina asked. She sat down next to her on the leather couch and swung her legs onto the hassock.

"He wanted to talk to Father Felix. There was estate stuff that needed to be settled." She tapped her clove against Dad's ashtray, a beer bottle melted so it looked like a life raft. She said, still staring into the screen, "He wanted some time by himself."

"I see."

"Sometimes I think love is an emotion best felt alone." Louise laughed, maybe a little too hard, as if to say she was sorry. "What did you do today?"

"I bought a funeral dress with Saul. It's really cute. If you want, I can show it to you later."

"Okay."

"Would it be okay if we made up?"

"Sure. Do you want to hear a bit of my screenplay?" Louise asked.

Marina nodded.

"Exterior, night. Enter Margaret, in a pale blue suit dress cut above the knee, from an airplane. She is greeted by Fidel Castro."

The doorbell rang.

I went to get the door, leaving the two of them in the living room.

Richard and Andreas were standing at the door.

Richard's eye was black. He said he'd been looking for me.

"Good news. Urethra Franklin would like to meet you. I spoke to Rob this morning about you, and he would like to propose a creative venture. We're late for the show. We may have already missed it."

"What happened to your eye?"

"Oh," he said and turned to Andreas, who was still in his

black leather vest, his arms folded. "Your father hit me. We had a disagreement. But now, now everything is good."

We were on our way to the city, to the Franklin concert. Marina rolled down the window in the back. They were yelling back and forth to each other in the backseat, with Andreas stuck in the middle, looking on gamely. Richard sat in front, inspecting his eye in the vanity mirror.

"The band wants to meet you," he said. "I've described you to them, mentioned your resemblance. They're intrigued; this is natural. They want to extend their condolences. Do you sing?"

The thought made me giggle. I had no musical ability whatsoever. I remember my father's efforts to teach me guitar ended badly, with my fingers raw and my feelings hurt. I was eleven and had wanted to learn—back then I still admired my father and his porky, callused fingers. I couldn't sing.

"They think they can turn you into a recording star. Their new single is not doing so well. They want your voice on a remixed version."

I asked Richard why my father hit him.

"Your father," he said, "thinks I have been asking too much of him. I interviewed him again this afternoon, and he thinks my questions are impolite. I said I needed total exposure. He said our cash arrangement did not specify total exposure."

"Cash arrangement?"

"Yes, a sum was exchanged in return for exclusive information, including his interview." He turned off the vanity-mirror light and flipped back up the passenger-seat sun visor. His long legs were pushed against the glove compartment. "You notice I haven't asked to speak to you today."

I nodded, figuring this to be the windfall my father came upon that allowed him to pay for his house renovations, the burial costs. Yet something remained unsettled. I felt a little dizzy.

Richard chuckled. Then he removed an envelope from his jacket pocket. "I have decided to let you come to me."

I opened Richard's envelope. It was unsealed and inside was a cashier's cheque for ten thousand dollars. I held it up, so that I could see it in the halogen white lights of the cars behind us.

"Keep it," Richard said. "Hold on to it and let me know your decision by Sunday—no, Monday."

Meanwhile Louise had decided, while we listened to Neil Young's *Rust Never Sleeps*, that rock and roll had indeed died.

"But it's always been an art form that had a low originality quotient," Marina was arguing, "sprung from primeval longing. It follows a long-standing tradition of white guys wishing they were black. British guys really wishing they were sharecroppers."

"I guess what I mean is that rock and roll is no longer a mass movement, the soundtrack to large-scale opposition," Louise said. "It's come to an end, the fire-sale point of rock and roll's history. What we have instead is cannibalism in pop music. Bands used to steal guitar licks off their albums. Now they sample them, they delete vocal tracks and punch in drum tracks and loop bass lines. They settle lawsuits over copyright infringements."

"My stepbrother's obsession in high school was with live albums," Marina said. "*Live at Leeds, The Song Remains the Same, After the Flood, Live Rust, Loco Live, Live at Winterland, Frampton Comes Alive.* Bootlegs galore. He didn't even go to any concerts on account of some phobia or another, but he had to have the live albums. Every day, I'd walk past his music and hear the roar of the crowd.

"Strange guy, my stepbrother," Marina added. "He died, drowned in the bathtub when I was fourteen, two years after his dad divorced my mom."

"Christ, you never told me that," Louise said. "What happened?"

"He was testing scuba gear."

We were late. By the time we got into the city, to the east-side stadium in which the Franklins performed, we had missed their entire performance, not that I minded, but Richard and Andreas needed footage from the show for a segment about the Canadian tour. We parked the car behind the stadium, watching young girls and older men streaming out of the stadium wearing Urethra Franklin T-shirts and Urethra Franklin hemp bracelets, passing information booths on reproductive rights and logging treaties in glossy pamphlets.

Richard stood at an entrance talking to an assistant leaning against a turnstile, a clipboard clamped against her chest. She followed Richard to the car.

The assistant crouched down to the car window, her laminated ID card dangling from her neck. She seemed to recognize me. I turned off the car radio.

"We've been waiting for you," she said.

"Come," Richard said, "we are going backstage."

"How many of you are there?" the assistant asked him.

"Four."

"Fine," she said, removing four laminates from her clipboard. "Let's go."

The assistant told me she was a big fan, just that, as if I'd done something special. She introduced herself, but I forgot her name immediately—I was getting good at that. We turned off the engine and followed her along the lot to a fenced area behind the building where the tour buses were parked, shining sleek and silver. She nodded at two security guards as we passed the rear entrance. The backstage area was all cement and ugly piping, lent a dull pallor by the fluorescent lights.

"They play hockey here, yeah?" Richard asked. "They play curling here, do they not?"

From the stage, there were cables being slung around the thick shoulders of men in overalls, speakers rolled along on carts.

There were couches against the walls and tables set up for a buffet and bar. There were musicians, a guy holding drumsticks with a towel around his neck and a skinny albino guy in a hard hat with tattoos running down his arms, milling around the open bar, eating crackers and drinking from plastic cups. Beside them were the Franklins' friends, the quiche-makers.

Richard wanted to know where Urethra Franklin was. The assistant pointed to a door at the far end of the room. Richard excused himself. He wanted to speak to the band alone first.

There was the radio personality from the press conference camped beside the oyster bar.

Ramona the VJ was sitting on a canvas folding chair. She was sipping from a bottle of water.

"Oh, look," Marina said. "There's our friend, the French tart."

"Hey, pedal pushers," Louise said, giggling. "Nice."

"What a fashion trendsetter."

"Or does she prefer the term 'capri pants'?"

"My goodness, it's the young camera man," Ramona said. "And look," she nodded at Marina, "you've brought your mother again. How is it you are here? You win a contest, eh? Meet the band. You save your bottle caps?"

The assistant put her hand on my elbow.

"He's a guest of honor. May I introduce to you Helena St. Pierre's son, Saul. Saul St. Pierre."

"I didn't know she had a son," Ramona said. "When did Helena St. Pierre find the time to have children? Who knew she had a son? Who knew she had sex? I thought the woman was a saint."

I just nodded dumbly. Marina was standing by the oyster bar pretending to gag.

"Well," the assistant said, "don't you think the resemblance is amazing?"

"Who are his friends?" Ramona said, nodding at Dad's houseguests.

The assistant shook her head.

"I don't have any information about them."

Ramona sat with one leg up against the canvas chair's arm. In her lap was her video camera. She raised the chunky machine onto her shoulder and pointed her microphone at me, still sitting in her folding chair.

"You must have felt horrible the last few days. Tell French Canada how you are feeling."

"Well, you know"—pausing, as I made my first public statement—"someone died. My mother is dead." It came out sounding as though I were a zombie.

"Yes, right. How did you find out? How did you receive such information?"

Her eyes were set wide and her mouth fell open, revealing comely white teeth and pink gums. She had a flirty look on her face, this haze of arousal fogging her eyes, I thought, my stomach dropping as I came upon a dirty realization of my own.

The dressing-room door cracked open. Richard waved me in.

I excused myself from Ramona. I felt numb and angry and pissed off and wired. Marina was watching me from the corners of her eyes, frowning in a way that made her look less pretty. I moved past the musicians and roadies and managers and disc jockeys and into the Urethra Franklin dressing room, all leather couches and leafy plants and baskets of fruit. There was bottled water chilling in a huge ice bucket. The members of the band broke out in applause when they saw me, as if I were the one who had just given a concert. Richard, his right eye puffy and purple, clamped a hand on my shoulder and was set to introduce me to the band individually when I asked him how much he paid my father for Helena St. Pierre's address.

Sunday

The big blowup came that afternoon in the living room. I found him in his recliner, already dressed for the viewing. He was in a dark blue suit, the top button of his pressed shirt undone, a sleepy look on his face. His legs were crossed and in his open hand he held his tie, neatly folded, red with white stripes.

My father saw me and yawned.

"I wasn't expecting you."

I apologized out of reflex.

"There's no reason to say you're sorry. I was expecting someone else. And Marina—she's the one you're looking for, right—she's out this moment with Louise. I asked them both to go out for the day so I could be here by myself for a moment, at least until my guest arrives. I haven't had time to think."

I told him I needed to ask him something.

"Ask me anything," he said sweetly. "You're my son." My

father had an arsenal of complicated expressions. Like this one—this sweet, gentle look on his face. He could blindside me with unexpected demonstrations of generosity and compassion. This was called charm.

"First, sit down," he said. "You're making me nervous."

It was in the air, I thought. Fatigue in the room like humidity. A jungle of exhaustion. Dad coughed into a fist and cleared his throat. I could tell he wasn't in the mood to listen, that his reedy voice, so whiny and ironical, was already craggy from talking. I sat on the far end of the couch away from him.

"I don't know if they're going to be here much longer, Saul. I'm talking about my houseguests. Louise Gordon and Marina Finch. They're nice girls. They're smart girls. But they'll be gone sooner than you think. Women. They land where the wind blows. I'm saying this now for you to keep in mind in case you're becoming attached. I know, I know, you have something to say, though I feel obliged to speak my piece first. Age before beauty. I mean, they are beautiful young women, and it is nice to be appreciated, to be the object of appreciation, but I'm going to have to ask them to leave soon because there's been too much excitement. It's fucking with my health. I can't shit properly. And if it's been many laughs having them around, it's been so with the knowledge that it isn't forever. Not that forever means anything. Cockroaches live forever. Your name on a marker and your piece-of-shit car and your kitchen and your cheap-o hit single. We can't expect perfection to last more than seconds, minutes. You remember perfect moments like you sense the oven is on.

"I admit to being a poor father. But it's not been because I haven't cared about you. I tried and I tried. I got tired. It wasn't what I was suited for. But now you're eighteen years old, you can

pretty much do as you please. You can hate me to your heart's
fill, but you've turned out well, in any case. Perhaps in spite of
me. Eighteen. I cared about you as much as I could. I got tired.
Your mother had worn me out by the time you were born. You
know how the saying goes: I'd rather go to jail than fall in love
again. Set your clock by those words. I don't speak from lofty vis-
tas, from blissful, snowcapped mountaintops, Saul, no, but from
the gutter. She was the only person I have ever loved, fully and
voluntarily. I tried to take her suffering and make it my own. I
tried to see the world through her eyes. I did my utmost to give
her what she wanted, but what she said she wanted didn't please
her. We argued, we yelled and slept around on one another, we
drank and did coke and pills, we spent entire weeks apart and
got people who worked for us to relay hurtful messages. One
night she said she wanted to leave me. I said she couldn't, I for-
bade it, and I sent her to the doctors in Montreal. The doctors
talked to her and their diagnosis was that she wanted to leave
me. All right, fine. I realized I couldn't keep her. So I told her to
go. I told her she shouldn't feel obliged to stay. But then she
decided, after stalling for a month, sleeping in another room,
even packing her bags, that she didn't want to go anymore. She
wanted a child instead, something she'd wanted but gave up on.
Of all decisions to make. I went along with her to make her
happy. You don't tell a woman what she wants, even if you might
know better. If you're smart, you agree, you roll your eyes, then at
night you kick the blankets from her feet.

"So she got pregnant after us trying for a year. She adored
you. It made me jealous how she doted on you. I said we
needed to tour again and she thought it was a good idea, but
when we did, it put her in a black mood, the blackest. She said

she hated me. I told her again to go and again she begged me not to let her. She couldn't keep her answers straight. I was tired; I had no heart. Not to say I wasn't surprised when she actually ran off, that she actually did. I'm sorry, Saulie."

"When did you get her address?"

He tilted his head a little and raised his eyebrows. The warmth on his face disappeared, some gear inside him turned, even as that little smile struggled afloat on his face. He continued in the same level tone.

"Richard told you that, did he? That's your question?" He laughed. *"Saul"*—looking at me incredulously—"I could always get her address if I'd wanted to. If you had bothered to ask me, I would have given it to you—for free. If you weren't so lazy, so self-absorbed. You should already know that. Don't waste my time. Don't be so fucking stupid. People asked me where she was and I said I didn't know. I was being honest, but they assumed that I couldn't find her—I only had to make a phone call. She would get mail, cheques, for a few years after the fact, after her so-called mysterious disappearance. I mailed those to her grandmother—you never met her. She didn't want to see you. I sent the divorce papers to the old woman. Her grandmother, your great-grandmother, received them until she died a few years back, then those two idiot cousins—you may have seen them on TV, Ricky and Ezra, those morons with their quiches and roadblocks—complaining about how bad they have it, when they lived quite nicely off Helena. Put fatty through culinary college. Leni didn't want a penny, and they took advantage of her. Ricky and Ezra. They wanted to speak tonight at the viewing. I listed the many ways they could fuck off.

"I had known she was in Bangkok for years. Before she died, her grandmother wrote me saying Helena was in Asia and that it was my marital obligation to make things right. It wasn't until maybe a year ago that I heard from her. Helena called me, asking about you. In case you're wondering, she wanted to know how you were. She asked to speak to you. When I told her I wouldn't allow it, she said that it was all right, she said she had forgiven me, prayed that I had turned to righteousness. She called in the middle of the night. Jana asked me who it was. I wouldn't say and we argued about that because she's always been a jealous woman. Then I hit her. That was the night your stepmother decided to leave me. In case you're keeping track of the score."

Dad yawned again, his mouth closing on a small burp. "I never sent her any mail. And so I thought that was that. Then about a month ago, she wrote me. She heard her own voice on the radio. Someone, a little whore she was teaching English, had recognized her. She asked me what I could do. Can you believe it? There was nothing to be done. She was furious. 'I won't have it,' she said. As belligerent as always. 'I won't have it.' She accused me of profiting on her pain. I did no such thing, but it gave me the idea. The return address was written on the envelope. I admit it—one reason I let Richard on her was to see what had become of her. I wanted to hear what she had to say. Maybe after all these years I had become curious. I've had people looking at me sideways, thinking nasty thoughts about me, surmising. Oh, hell, I thought. Richard wanted to hear my side of the story—at least I thought he did. It turns out he's no good, either. There were so many people sniffing around for an interview, who wanted to find Helena, and sooner or later they would have found her, with or without my assistance. I figured I may as well get a paycheque out of it."

"Where is it?"

"I put it in the bank."

"The letter she sent you?"

"No, the cheque."

"What about the letter?"

Dad groaned, out of impatience. "I threw it in the trash, Saul. Just like the note Felix brought with him, the one they found in her flat. I burned that without even opening it. Oh, don't look at me like that. *Don't.* Not in my house. It was addressed to me and I saw fit to burn it."

My father sighed. He closed his eyes for a moment, before they fluttered back open. He stood up and turned his back to me, he buttoned his top button, he ran the red striped tie along the back of his neck, he slipped the tie underneath his starched white collar, he knotted his tie, then fastened it, wiggling his ass. Then he sat down, in his suit, looking toward the floor, a fan on the coffee table whipping back his hair.

I got up and started out of the room. I stopped at the kitchen entrance.

"You're a liar."

"Well, yes, Saulie, I am an inveterate liar," he said, his voice singsong and mocking. "What have I said that sounds untrue? You tell me."

"You never let her go," I said.

"Of course, she left on her own."

"You were too weak to keep her."

"Oh, right. Now I remember. I was too weak."

"She ran off with another man."

"Yes, she did. An old friend of hers. The guy with the book. The book everyone's talking about." Then he added, "Strange how Leni's death buoys us all up."

"She never loved you."

Dad nodded.

"You're right, that's very possible. She didn't." He picked a piece of lint from his slacks, held it up to his face, then watched it fall to the floor. "Is that all? I'm expecting company."

"She despised you. She thought you were vile and despicable. She left without warning because if you knew she was leaving, you would've asked her to take me along."

"Don't be melodramatic. *Please.*"

"But she left without me. You couldn't control her. Your career depended on her voice, her stage presence, otherwise you'd still be working at a shoe store in Winnipeg. You thought you were doing it for her, but she didn't care about the music or the money, the things you got your kicks from. She loathed it. You did everything you could to keep her. You put her on anti-depressants, you told her she had contractual obligations to fulfill, you got her pregnant. You thought this was devotion, yet she loved someone else, and it made you bitter, it turned you angry and cheap."

We heard the doorbell ring, but Dad didn't move out of his seat. He let me finish, if not to humor me then because he was afraid. By now I was trembling, my voice cracking. I sounded stupid, like a TV detective, like a lawyer giving his final argument: I know, I know. But this was what I said. "It made you vengeful. And then you had your opportunity."

We heard the door unlocking.

"Are you finished?" my father said. "Am I free to go?"

"You're responsible for her death."

Jana appeared at the other end of the kitchen.

"Saul," she said. "I wasn't expecting you here."

"That's what Dad said."

"Your father wanted to show me the kitchen."

She was staring at the hole in the ceiling, opening and clos-ing the newly installed cabinets.

Dad brushed by me at the kitchen entrance.

Jana glared at him.

"What were you yelling about?"

"The same old. Saul was only putting me in my place. Giv-ing me a regular tongue-lashing. I think I've been grounded. I can't leave the house for two weeks. My car privileges have been suspended."

"There you go again. This is a tough time for him. He needs your guidance. He's curious about his past. But what do you do? You joke. You make light of his pain. You stick your thing into little tarts. This is no way for a man your age to act."

"We were talking about the boy's mother. I suppose you were the one who filled his head with this nonsense."

"What nonsense?"

"That I was responsible for all this business," he said. "Look at him—he wants to hit his own father."

"I was telling him," I said to Jana, "what you told me."

Dad glared at me, his eyes dark and narrow, disgust crawling across his face, a pitch-black scowl.

"And what did Jana tell you?" he asked. "What does Jana know about what happened?" He blinked. "Not a thing. Which means you know considerably less than nothing. I suppose it's easier to blame me. It was the same with your mother, and I imagine her hysteria passed into your blood. That's one thing you got from her."

Jana turned to me, her arms crossed. She thought it was time for me to go home.

The phone was ringing when I got home.

"Don't ask me how I got your phone number," said a man on the line. "I asked a couple of people; a friend of mine is an ex-detective. I had a brainstorm. I was watching the news when I thought, Where is her son? Because no one asks what the kids think. But aren't they the ones with stories to tell? Aren't all our best stories the ones we pick up from our parents as children in our formative years, little creepy stories we half remember?"

"Who are you?"

His name was Leslie Erickson. "I was flipping through your parents' biography, the one I wrote way back when. I'd looked at it and saw your picture, you on a sled, age three, and I wondered, He must be of adult age right now. Knowing what I know about your parents' lives, there was so much I had to leave out, I bet you had an interesting childhood. Listen: how well do you do in your English classes? I mean, do you know a run-on sentence, split infinitives? Do you keep a diary? Were you ever abused? We can use that. You can tell me. Things you might think are perfectly harmless can seem hideously inhuman to others. Of course I can offer my services, over thirty years' experience in writing and editing, and then we can put it down, and you have your story—staring you in the face. If you want to appear in a national magazine, here it is. Don't worry if you think you're too unattractive for TV. There are plenty of heifers onscreen. Let me give you my number. I mean, this is an opportunity. It's a story. The world needs stories. Let me ask you—how would you like to leave your mark on the earth?"

I said I'd think about it.

"Have you been talking to anyone else? *Fuck me.* Who is it?"

I went upstairs. There were shoes, polished, at the foot of my bed. My suit laid out for me, slacks first, a coiled belt sitting on the fly, an ironed shirt placed over my jacket, both on hangers, the sleeves flung out, ready to embrace. A blue tie was slung around the jacket hanger.

I folded the clothes neatly on the back of a chair. I usually got eight hours of sleep a night, ten on weekends, back when I was moderately normal, I thought, as I stripped to my underwear and lay down.

I tried not to think about Helena St. Pierre. I tried not to think of squandered opportunities. Because maybe my father would have told me about her, her whereabouts, if only I had asked. That would be like my father, not to volunteer information, not for free, anyway. But I also figured that I had never really considered looking for my mother, that I was perhaps too lazy and unimaginative to seek her out, and that perhaps I secretly wanted her life to remain a secret. I had too much respect for mysteries. I was terrified of them.

I needed sleep. I would nap for a good hour, I decided. I would clear my head and think of pleasant things. I would dream about swimming in northern Ontario with my grand-parents; I would dream my favorite movies; I would dream about the great meals in my life, like the time I had really good Mexican or the very excellent Polish sausage of two weeks ago. I would dream about sex the way I did before I started having it, without responsibility, without foreplay, without smells and spills and sounds.

Instead, I lay in bed thinking about my book deal.

My autobiography would be something. It would be sad and tawdry, so brief it could be printed on a Bazooka bubble-gum wrapper for fifth graders who would also buy my forthcoming collaboration with Urethra Franklin. There would be a comic-book version of my memoir and a TV movie, which I'd insist on starring in. I'd play me and some guy with wavy hair would be my old man and we'd get that woman from the bikini-wax infomercial to be my dear departed mother. I would move to Hollywood, never to see anyone in this crummy town ever again, which was what I wanted all along.

Of course, the book would have to come first. I could see myself on the cover, a dumb frown on my face. It would be called *Child of Tragedy* or *Tears in Heaven: The Saul St. Pierre Story* or simply *Thanks, Dad*. I would get a ghostwriter, some-one literary, but it would only be me autographing copies at supermarkets and book fairs. I would appear on those television shows where they took callers. It would be one of those shows with a five-second broadcast delay, where the host would tell the caller to turn down his set because of the Matterhorn-type echo of selfsame delay, which they'd have in order to cut off callers who turned out to be foulmouthed or racist or crazy, so that the viewers at home wouldn't hear a single offensive word. Some caller would be swearing at me, but they'd only see their host saying something like, "I guess he hung up," and me smil-ing like a bemused, mentally retarded mannequin.

The phone began to ring. I fantasized hearing my mother's voice on the other end from the netherworld, purring an apology. I dove for the phone.

Navi was on the line: "Where have you been? You missed all the excitement."

"When?"

"On Friday, when we occupied the principal's office. It was great. I wish you were there. They had to call in policemen in riot gear. We were all carried out, lame-duck style. They put handcuffs on me and took down all our names and asked us never to set foot on school property. Some guy spit on a cop and was put in a holding cell. We had coverage on three different stations in the Lower Mainland and a spot on CBC Newsworld—the quiche thing had broken up by then. I think we really made a point."

"About what?"

"Exactly."

I told Navi how I met Urethra Franklin last night.

"They want to put my voice on record. The proceeds would go to collective presses in Montreal and The Hague. I haven't decided whether I'll do it. I don't know. What do you think of their music?"

"My sisters like it a lot."

"Well, they're huge with eighth graders."

"The drummer's kind of cute."

"I met her, too. Her name's Dorit. She's sort of bloated in real life."

"I like round girls."

I checked the clock radio on my night table. I needed to be at the funeral home in an hour. I sat up in my bed and began to get dressed.

"Have you talked to Rose lately?" I asked Navi. I had the phone wedged between my ear and shoulder as I slid on my pants.

"Why don't you just call her?"

"Not likely. We have a viewing for the body tonight."

"I know. I saw it on the news."

"I'm pretty good, actually."

"I've been worried about you."

"I'm pretty good."

I was feeling lighthearted, oddly enough. Almost giddy. It was almost over. They'd have put her body in the ground by tomorrow afternoon, and then everyone would leave, Richard and Andreas, Louise and Marina, and practically everything would be as it was before. I would get to sleep and maybe Rose would return my calls. I would attend classes so I might have a chance of passing my exams. All this business would calm down.

I put on my jacket. There was a full-length mirror on my door so I inspected myself. My tie was a little crooked and I needed gel in my hair, but otherwise I was looking pretty sharp. I appeared somber and sincere, maybe a little too serious. I made a goofy face. I flipped my eyelids inside out and smiled with all my teeth and gums. I started throwing punches in front of the mirror.

"I bet you didn't know I've been offered a book deal for my life story."

"Cool," Navi said. "I've been writing mine since the age of eleven."

This was probably true. On a wall in Navi's room, next to his framed honor roll certificates, was a picture of Subcommandante Marcos, leader of the Zapatista movement in Chiapas,

Mexico, that he took off the Internet—two eyes staring forth from a ski mask. Subcommandante Marcos was Navi's idol. For an English composition assignment last year, Navi wrote a surprisingly humorless short story about how he was actually Marcos's only son, conceived while the Samra family was on vacation in Oaxaca in 1980. In the story, Marcos—disguised as a friendly Jesuit priest and tour guide—kidnaps Mrs. Samra. He places his finger over the lips of Navi's mother, and they disappear into the hills outside town for "re-education." What followed in Navi's story was surprisingly indecent, considering the woman in the story was supposedly his mother.

In our own ways, Navi and I both dreamed of more auspicious origins.

I was waiting by the door when Jana got home. "Give me five minutes," she said. And she kept her word, much to my surprise. She came bounding down the stairs in a hat and a dark suit dress with white buttons running down the middle, a sun-bleached expression on her face. We were both in a bright mood, it seemed.

We climbed into the car. Its seats were warm, the air inside felt like melted rubber, and I was getting hot in my suit. I rolled down the window and wished for air-conditioning. Jana put her key to the ignition. We started out of the complex driving lot, our heads bobbing as the car went over the parking lot's speed bumps.

"It's the kitchen I wanted."

We were on Trunk Road when we pulled over to let a fire truck pass by.

"Your father wants you to move back in with him."

"I won't," I said.

"He thinks it might be better."

"What about you, then?"

"He thinks I should move back, too."

"You can't," I said. "You two are divorced."

"*Saul.*"

"Christ, why does everybody say that? Do people have trouble with my name?"

The fire truck was out of eyeshot now. Jana pulled back into traffic.

"I thought you were marrying Dale," I said. "All of a sudden, he's out of the picture. Have you thought about him at all?"

"Yes," Jana snapped back. Her left-turn blinker was still on, making its clicking sound. There was something wrong with the car's blinker and it didn't automatically turn off. It clicked like a panting dog.

"Your blinker's on."

"Oh." She turned it off. "Of course I've thought about Dale. I think about Dale. I've given thought. And it's not as though I've come to any decision yet. For either of them. I never gave Dale an answer, and I haven't given your father one either. But it's not that simple." She paused. "Ian's different."

"What do you mean by that?"

"It means that, for him, I'm willing to do things I'll regret later."

"Sounds kind of lousy."

"It is."

"Do you want my advice, Jana?"

Jana smiled, then nodded patronizingly.

"Don't act rashly."

Jana laughed. We both laughed.

"Okay," she said.

Jana liked to tell the story about how I ran into her arms the very first time I saw her, when I came to live with her and Dad. We were at the airport, my grandmother was holding me by my collar, my grandmother who might have had a sweet face but was a bitch on wheels, more impatient than my grand-father—that was how my father was raised, and it explained a lot. She was saying how shy a four-year-old I was, but before she could even make her warning, I had pried myself away from her dry, bony hand. It was 1984, three and a half years after the St. Pierres ended. Jana wasn't sure whether she would be a good mother, a good mother figure, to a boy too swift and will-ful for Ian's arthritic parents. She was only twenty-two and the youngest child in her family—her two older sisters had already moved out of the house before she was even in grade school. She was not even used to being married quite yet, not used to calling herself a wife.

And I came to her, she said, in tiny denim overalls, a half-Indian boy with watery eyes and a bowl cut, full of misplaced love. I placed my hands on her round cheeks.

As she told it, I kissed her square on the lips, and her heart melted.

We stopped at an intersection right before the funeral home. I could hear a lawn mower buzzing in the distance, out of view. "You're looking good today." She watched me, this dreamy glaze over her eyes. "Helena would be proud to have such a beautiful son. It would make her feel better about herself." The car started moving. "She was a vain woman, Saul. She was deeply infatuated with herself. You'd figure if you spent your life obsessed with yourself, you'd pick up an insight or two. Well, not the case. You should know that. Don't look for explanations. She was plain dumb, is all."

"Stupid people should know better."

"They should."

I raised my fist in the air and shook it. "Stupid people, when will you learn?"

We entered the chapel from the rear, to the row reserved for the immediately bereaved, where my father sat alone, the pew that allowed an unobstructed view of the open coffin and the floral arrangements encircling it like some Druid monument. Middle-aged heads turned, as if by cue, from practice and teamwork and cunning, when we approached. Neither of my parents had much family left, none who showed up. The mourners here were friends of my parents, musicians from Yorkville: family friends from out of town whom I'd met on a few occasions, all nice folks who played music at one time or another, a little loopy from too much prescription medication for joint inflammations and antisocial tendencies, who suffered from deafness in one ear and ringing sensations in the other. They were men in deerskin vests and bolo ties, wearing graying lamb-chop burns, wiry guys with high foreheads and forearms lined with veins, session players who followed their own style, all skinny leather ties and short-sleeved cotton shirts and scraggly facial hair, single earrings and sweatbands on stage, a dress code for rockers in mid-life as rigid as a street gang. They brought their wives, floppy-breasted women carrying big handbags. The room was full. They'd been waiting for this: they'd taken days off and driven eighteen hours straight or caught standby flights.

There was a volume swell at our entrance, my entrance. I was recognized, their eyes locking onto me as they tried to locate that resemblance, the love-child aura that followed me like the smell of a ripe egg. They mumbled about me over the sound of the pianist as she played in a corner, blocked from view by a halo of carnations. This lasted precisely one moment, hardly two bars of the organist's tune. Soon enough, the eyes of the room resettled on my mother's body in front of us, lying in a sleek silver coffin with black panels and brass handles along its sides, next to the podium. She was the centerpiece, a fig-urine, a drowsy debutante, her lips and cheeks rouged, her hair swept back, in her farewell performance.

Dad was talking to Father Felix, who stood crouched over him, his long body casting a shadow across Dad, who peered up at him. Felix moved back to the podium and began shuffling papers. Jana sat between us. She leaned over and whispered something into Dad's ear. He smiled.

There was a box of tissue next to me on the pew.

I could hear sniffling, mixed with the general mumble of the crowd. Programs folded and unfolded, asses sliding down pews, investments divulged softly.

I turned around and looked for people I knew. I searched until I found Marina and Richard by the wall, four rows back. They waved at me. Marina was wearing a black sleeveless number, her hair in pigtails, her arms creamy white.

I started to stand up for a better view of the body.

Jana looped a hand around my elbow and pulled me back into my seat.

Father Felix cleared his throat into the mike.

"In the name of the Father, the Son and the Holy Spirit."

We said the Lord's Prayer. I mouthed along from memory, though I didn't know where I'd had the chance to learn it. We weren't a religious family, not even my grandparents, who were nominally Catholic and went to Mass regularly out of respect for their parents' memory. I thought of belief in God as a demonstration of a child's love for his mother and father. I didn't think about Him, not usually, only when I was frightened, because I figured hell was a reasonable concept. We had jails in real life. We had punishment. We tortured.

When weren't hymns ugly business; when weren't they saccharine, up-tempo numbers? They were entirely unconvincing. Jana held her program up beside me so we could both sing from the lyrics printed, but I felt compelled to keep my mouth closed, my eyes on the coffin. My mother had been in the choir in Thailand. I imagined her singing these words. She must have really lost her marbles. Either it was a chemical imbalance or some tricky recessive gene, maybe even the Holy Spirit itself taking residence in her heart. But to end up singing this by her own free will—she might as well have stayed with my father.

Heaven had no local equivalent.

Dad was holding up well. He was practically barking out the words to the hymns, just as he did the Our Father. He snuck glances at the coffin. He dug his hands in his pockets, his shoulders hunched inward, his chin dropping to his chest.

The hymns went by slowly. I rocked back and forth on my feet.

There was Dad, Jana and I, together. There was Dad and my mother reunited. There was my mother and I, together at last, before the chapel audience. It was like a cruel TV show, something Richard might have hosted back in Germany, where secret guests lurked backstage in soundproof rooms and curtains drew open to reveal kitchen appliances. In that case, my mother was a dummy prize, a parting gift. A small brown face, a young woman's face, her cheeks hollow and her tiny nose rounding up on a blunt point, and her hair glossy black, her neck long and thin and framed by the frilly collar of the white summer dress she was to be buried in. I wanted to touch her. I wondered whether I would have the nerve to touch the body. I allowed myself to think dark thoughts.

Gord spoke first, reading from a piece of creased loose-leaf.

"I see a lot of familiar faces in the audience, and it's nice to see everyone again after all these years, even under these circumstances. Everyone here is looking prosperous. And much wiser." A few in the audience chuckled. Gord smiled briefly. "When Ian asked me to say something about her, I was left scratching my head about what to talk about. I really didn't know her too well for someone who played in her band for six years, not as well as I would have liked. She was quiet and let Ian speak for her, she let the music speak for her. But I know she was a kind woman who treated everyone on the road or in the studio with respect. She wasn't stuck up at all for such a big star, and we all know a lot of stuck-up musicians." More laughter. "She cared about people. I remember her being a good mother who was very proud of her son when he was born. From what I hear, she was a religious woman, and she treated the poor with the same sort of, um, compassion that I saw in her all those years ago. In fact, my wife Nadine and I have decided to name our first child after Helena." Gord broke into a smile;

some people chuckled. He nodded, then stepped away from the podium red-faced, people congratulating him when he sat down.

The other speakers who followed him didn't say much different. There were more people from the band, a couple who even knew my mother back in the Yorkville days. Their memories were fuzzy. They talked about Helena St. Pierre the libertine, the artist, the singer with a social conscience, but this was old news. I had heard it all before. I felt jilted.

It was my father's turn to speak. He ambled up, took a quick peek at the body, and then settled at the lectern, his hands gripping its sides.

I stood up to leave.

"Saul, sit down," Jana said, her face severe, a little impatient.

"I'm sorry."

My father watched me go without saying a word. I moved down the aisle and out of the chapel, keeping my eyes to the ground.

Mr. Dirk, the funeral guy, in the same dark suit, stood in the reception area with a couple of young female assistants, busy arranging a large metal coffee dispenser and trays of biscuits on tables.

Mr. Dirk looked up from the table.

"Sir, is there a problem?"

I shook my head.

"Refreshments will be ready in another ten minutes."

I nodded.

Mr. Dirk turned away, and as though she had been hiding behind him, Louise appeared, weeping in the corner of the room. She was wearing a man's dark short-sleeve shirt. Her lips were shiny from gloss. She held in her hands a ball of crumpled beige tissue.

"I thought he was brilliant," she was saying in between sobs.

"I'm sorry." I held out my hand, placing it on her elbow. This was what Jana usually did, before she drew someone into an embrace.

"I know why you're upset with him," she said. "I know why."

"It's okay," I said. I began to pull her toward me. She leaned against my bony chest and quaked.

"He wanted Helena to come out of hiding. A real live TV reunion. Asshole." She dabbed a ball of tissue against her eyes. We could hear the whiny, excitable voice of my father inside the chapel, pleading his case, memorializing a woman he loathed. "I'm so stupid. I'm so—I'm so disappointed."

I nodded. I knew how she felt. I really did. I knew what it was like to admire Ian St. Pierre. There was a time when I wanted to walk like him, to grow out my hair like him, to have the same sweaty callused fingers. I loved him to pieces. I loved my father for his best qualities: his wit, his determination, his laughter, even his occasional kindnesses. When he was at his best, I wanted him to be like that all the time. And it killed me that I wasn't good enough, not worth the trouble, for him to feel the same about me. It slayed me. My mother was my first unrequited love, but my father was a close second. I knew exactly how Louise felt.

A lawn mower rolled out of the parking lot from a shed next to the mausoleum. The lawn mower was green with yellow trim and yellow hubcaps. The driver was a man in a pair of overalls who wore safety goggles and big headphones. I sat outside the chapel, on a park bench in the garden with ruffly purple flow-ers and a pond, watching the mower rumble down the paved roads that crisscrossed the cemetery's lawns until it turned out of eyeshot. The man beside me on the bench was sucking on a cigarette in a dark sports jacket, a white shirt and black tuxedo pants, glossy gray lines running down each pant leg. His hair was receding and cautiously combed forward and he wore tinted wire-rims that fell to the end of his nose. On his jacket was an "It Takes Two to High-Five" button.

Nathan pushed his glasses up his nose with his pinky finger.

"Why aren't you inside?" I asked.

"I got chicken."

"You're my mother's old boyfriend."

He nodded.

"She left my dad for you."

He had this sick look on his face.

"No, she just left."

Even then he dressed as though he'd lost a bet. It wasn't the clothes that drew my mother to the man thirty years ago. Back when they first met, he looked ridiculous in his paisley shirts, chasing the zeitgeist's slippery tail. By the time they were in Toronto, he was all clean cut and geeky, like some Korean orphan brought back by missionaries, wearing Salvation Army handouts. He was this clumsy Chinese kid with a sharp mouth and a beau-tiful native girlfriend. She liked him because he was, in private, timid and sweet. He was twenty, two years older than she. She was his first. Intimacies aside, he kept his distance. He didn't drink like Ian would and he wasn't as much an asshole, but he was sometimes arrogant and willful to the point of whininess.

There was a wiriness to his body, a tenseness in his behavior, which was arousing. When she tickled him on the couch, he would wrestle her down and it seemed as if he took it a little too seriously. Sometimes she could picture him hitting her.

In Toronto, they lived in a second-story room in Kensington above a bakery. He worked at his uncle's restaurant, stealing singles and change from the till, reading newspapers, on the toilet downstairs or on an upturned milk crate in the back alley, left over from the breakfast rush. It was only a matter of time until his uncle fired him, until the Chinese family goodwill expired, but he was hanging on to the easy work as long as he could.

Nathan taught Leni Sinclair what she knew about ambition. Namely, that she required some. "If you're going to get anywhere," he said, half joking, "you'll need someone to run your life. And maybe lose five pounds." He had Hemingway as a cub reporter in mind when he decided to move to Toronto. At night, for an entire year, she watched him punching away at the vainglorious Olivetti Mondays through Saturdays, pulling sheets out of the machine and penciling in margin notes.

He sat near the edge of his wicker-backed chair, in slippers, narrow ankles crossed, in search of the next word, wriggling like a blind black man in front of his piano.

It's just annoying, she thought, this so-called dedication. It was Protestant and uptight and self-denying and everything she wasn't about.

He hated the books she read: Kerouac, Hesse, the Brautigan pocket editions, *Selected Quotations of Chairman Mao*. The plays of Joe Orton. They never saw the end to most of the movies they went to because he insisted on storming out halfway through. Antonioni and *Sansho the Bailiff* and Godard, that Swiss cunt who liked beginnings, middles and ends, though not necessarily in that order.

Leni liked everything she saw; she was an enthusiast, an avid participant, before her meltdown years later. She liked to wear a green Yugoslavian embroidered blouse, back when Yugoslavian fashion had a looser grip on the public imagination. She got the blouse from a friend who said she'd stolen it from the costume closet of the Chatham Little Theatre.

She volunteered at a co-op gallery next to a coffeehouse.

Art wasn't supposed to be drudgery. It was play. You lived art; you lived your life as art. It was detergent advertising copy and *Blondie* with the bubbles whited out and filled in with British cuss words and sound collage and party chat transcripts and recontextualized underwear hung on lines by orange plastic pegs.

He wouldn't even let her read his book.

She began to leave the house without him.

Somebody at the gallery needed help with his boat, so a group of them went over to paint its underside one weekend.

Another person brought a guitar. She impressed fellow boat painters by singing "Greensleeves," then "Sugar Mountain" and "Norwegian Wood."

He was not pleased about nude modeling, livid when she did it in public. He went to her happening, to see her spread out on the divan, airing her naughty bits on a downtown street, because she asked him to and almost threw punches at some hooting men, almost hit Ian St. Pierre. He paid off her fine with his stolen tips.

He thought she wasn't contributing enough to the household economy.

She thought the book was secretly about her.

She wanted to be an artist.

She wanted to reinvent it—the world.

She wanted to sing.

He thought she was loose.

One afternoon, the Greek landlady is on her knees planting mousetraps in the hall. "Your husband is out looking for you," the old woman says, without bothering to look up. "Or maybe he say he is going to Chinese restaurant. I don't know. Don't bother me. I am busy woman."

Leni unlocks the door and finds herself alone in their messy house with the manuscript lying around.

She's shocked by how little he knows about her, how she's portrayed, alternately, as shrew and fool.

She is halfway through when he comes in.

She throws a telephone at him.

To start, he says, it's not about you.

It's like a diary.

Secondly, you're not supposed to be reading this. This is private.

Then you admit—it is a diary.

You're invading my privacy.

She wags a finger like some prohibitionist marm, a figure of moral sobriety: You invaded mine first.

He follows her into the bedroom, where she's throwing her underwear in a knapsack.

You're a shithead. My grandmother was right about you.

Thirdly, you're only upset because it's honest.

She says she hates him, she says she's about to leave, a threat she's made before, one he doesn't take seriously since he's long stopped taking what she says seriously. Ian and Nathan would agree: she likes arguments and tantrums. It makes her face tingle in a nice way when she wails. She gets lost. She barely finds her way back home after she leaves the house. She just avoids getting on a bus to Etobicoke, wherever that is, that's how helpless and hopeless she is.

She hasn't said one word whether the book was any good.

Slut, he says. The space between them has been pregnant with that word.

Would it kill her to say one nice thing about the book?

You're a slut, he says. Go off and sleep around. Fuck everyone in the city.

He sits down at the kitchen and starts tapping away again at the typewriter, maybe because she hates its sound.

Whore.

The house smells like patchouli and a gerbil farm. There is an unfinished papier-mâché sculpture of a yak on the kitchen counter. There is a dying fern next to it. There is a mason jar half-filled with apple cider next to that. The light is depressing. Nathan said he hated being in direct sunlight. He's funny about a lot of things. She throws the typewriter off the table. It crashes against a chair, then smacks the ground with a metallic thud and ring. He grabs her by the arms, afraid for his stuff.

"You're going to hit me, aren't you?" she asks.

"No."

"Yes, you are."

It's as though she dares him, as though she doesn't think he's got it in him. It's a test and he has no choice but to follow through. He throws her to the ground—it's easier than he has thought it would be, and he's thought about it more than once—then lands his foot between a couple of ribs. It almost sounds like laughter when she screams. He hasn't even hurt her. He wants to kick her again, but then she really starts to wail, a scream like an angry tea kettle, like a startled cat, her hands in front of her face. She rolls away, flings herself against the arm of their upholstered loveseat.

The guy who owns the boat—Ned the painter—has already offered to put her up. She's been thinking this over. She takes her clothes, she takes her battered body and leaves.

Helena. Nathan listens to the radio and buys a couple of their records, listens to them on the armchair swirling the Cardhu in its tumbler, lingers over magazine photos, a *Rolling Stone* interview, described in another catatonic *Maclean's* spread, rereads the articles about her hospital stays for exhaustion, a piece about her having brunch with Abbie Hoffman in Montreal in 1976, but he doesn't think too much about her. Well, maybe a little. Once, in 1973 or '74, he watches Trudeau in a buckskin jacket on TV with his hippie wife and furrows his brow. There's something defiant in his vanity, a fussiness that softens his laser-guided political heart. Here he is, on television, blending in at a St. Pierres show in Ottawa. The first prime minister who can get mellow. His wife, Margaret, is some magical gift to his vanity.

In his bathrobe at one in the afternoon, he sorts through the mail, thinking, sarcastically, this is easy, this is the life, at the joy of daylight squandered. He picks up the newspaper.

But then he reads about the birth of her son, and he gets depressed. Saul St. Pierre, a New Year's child, 1980. The woman he knew wouldn't have had a child. What is wrong with her?

She looks less human every time a photo of her is published. She's gotten so thin. There's nothing in her eyes.

He decides to write to her. To the effect of: congratulations, remember me, I was thinking about you, anyway hope you're well, I'm doing fine, I remember that time, do you, maybe sometime, if you feel like it, we should get together, well, anyway, take care. He is too nervous to write anything very personal. He's surprised when she responds. They exchange notes. Then she calls him on tour, confides, confesses her unhappiness, her difficulties, people were whispering about it being post-partum depression, but she's *positive* that wasn't the case. They talk about child-rearing. They agree that the approach in that book, where you leave the kids wailing alone in their rooms all night, is too terrible to imagine. He hangs up when his wife—the sweet gentle woman who accepts his fear of the free enterprise system and pays the rent—awakens. It feels good, oddly good, invigorating. He feels guilty preemptively.

She suggests they meet at the Labor Day show. She's been planning her departure, hasn't told anyone about it. Go to Vancouver. There'll be a ticket for him at the entrance. After the show, he can give the road manager his name and she'll meet him. They can be alone and have coffee or something.

You need to come get me, she tells him.

"I need someone to write my memoirs," I said.

"So soon?" he asked.

"It's now or never, really."

"You could put pen to paper yourself," Nathan said. He stubbed his butt against the heel of his shoe. "They say it's therapeutic."

"Or you could do it for me."

"That's just laziness."

"Maybe."

"I don't even know you."

"Use your imagination," I said.

He smiled and shook his head.

"Now who's being lazy?"

He's on the floor, though he decides to stay away from the swell of flesh pressing against the stage. How long has it been since his last concert? It must've been years.

He doesn't like the smell of sweat, the stray elbows, the wolf whistles.

The roadies have finished setting up the stage, which remains empty a few minutes longer.

The crowd applauds.

She appears dressed in dark cowboy boots, a white skirt and a billowy white blouse with puffy sleeves. Her husband steps on stage wearing sunglasses. He wears his hair down to his shoulders. They both look thin, worn haggard from travel. She doesn't have that motherly glow, that glow— almost unreal, almost concocted, like a trial experiment from a research lab at Johnson and Johnson. The husband takes his place off in the back with the band, leaving her out front. She seems to acknowledge the crowd with a shy smile fluttering on her mouth.

He's only here on a lark; he's only lied to his family and made the four-hour flight to say hello. He's made no promises.

He moves into the crowd.

He wants to see the whites of her eyes.

She's two inches tall from where he's standing. They've made her prettier, put magenta eye shadow and lipstick on her, sprayed and molded her hair, bleached her teeth—which had already been capped. She's like a human jukebox, standing in front of the microphone, mouthing song after song. He's never heard her sing live before. It's a little husky and slightly off-key, something that takes people time to get used to. Her voice booms. It has a belly. It leaves a tread. He doesn't really know any of the songs. They're up-tempo country rock and lilting, buttery ballads that seem to melt into one another. She says very little to the audience, only polite thank yous and brief introductions to songs, but it comes off coquettish in her little-girl manner.

He's proceeding through the layers of people, most of whom move aside when he brushes against them. These are gentle folk. Some are dancing, all sway in one way or another. Some of the women hold their hands over their heads and dance in a self-consciously sexy way. He gets maybe fifteen feet from the stage, enough to see the spit from her mouth and her face beaten down by the stage lights—red, blue, purple. He's light-headed from the humidity.

He feels himself being swept up in awe. His spirit lifts from his body and settles on his shoulders for a better view. She looks good, entranced in the music and burrowing into herself, her eyes staring past the crowd. He tries to push further in, but it's harder going. The people in front of him have linked arms or something. These are diehards, the ones who feed off this proximity. He can see the logic. She's like a movie star, not a bombshell, but the actress who steals your heart, the one who plays the soiled, repentant woman in movie adaptations of

Russian novels, a star who inspires newfound domestic urges and your worst, most syrupy impulses, a perfectly soft-mouthed woman lit with a bar of moonlight across her face, whose onscreen tears cleave your heart.

She seems maybe to catch his face in the audience, or so he thinks. She looks down at the stage and finishes the tune.

Then she rushes off the stage, her husband's eyes following her suspiciously. Nathan starts away, sees a pair of security men at a side entrance by the gate and goes toward them. But the crowd around him isn't moving, nor are the lights back on. They are waiting for the encore.

Ten, twenty minutes pass and she hasn't appeared. A "bullshit" chant is started somewhere in the cheap seats. He remembers that documentary he saw about Altamont. Only a little while back he read about a woman who needed a fortune's worth of dental work when she was winged by a piece of guitar debris at a Who concert. He imagines little kids being pressed against a metal fence. He thinks like the parent he is and a wave of nausea briefly overtakes him. Some provinces have already banned festival seating. The people here, though, seem like responsible citizenry. A good age range, a lot of young couples, he thinks, suddenly feeling a little awkward about being by himself. He usually thinks twice about going to films alone when his wife is too tired. He definitely doesn't go out alone on Fridays or on statutory holidays. The band returns to the stage without her. The audience throws pennies and nickels at the band, some begin rushing the stage. They move all at once so they get by security. Ian comes back onstage, hopes are raised, until he walks off with a sour look on his face. People are mad. The gates get pushed over and people in front are stepped on as more advance. A guard slams a fist into the gut of one college-aged man trying to get to the drum set. Somebody jumps on the back of the guard, scratching his face.

There's a stampede in the other direction and more people are tripping into one another. Nathan stays calm, trying not to bump into anyone. He wonders what he'll say to her, where they'll go. He starts mouthing something for when they finally meet, when one security guard places a hand flat against his chest. Nathan gives him his name. He's expected backstage, he explains to him. The guard speaks into a walkie-talkie, repeating his name. He waits for an answer, then shakes his head.

Monday

Marina called the morning of the funeral. I gave her directions to my house on the phone and waited for her at the park outside our housing complex. Little kids were running around a jungle gym. Next to the swing set, a poodle rolled on the grass, its hind legs pedaling in the air. She approached from the opposite end of the park in a white tank top and khaki shorts. Her shoulders swayed and her heels scuffed the grass. There was something rubbery about her walk that I liked. It made her look young, my age.

"We had breakfast with your dad. Good old Ian. He gave us our walking papers, then he dumped the waffles on our plates. He wants us out by Wednesday. I wasn't surprised. Do you know what I'm saying? I've been getting that vibe. I'm happy to get going, in fact. Louise wants to leave soon—this afternoon, maybe. She's not taking it well. She thinks it's something she did. Don't look at me like that. Of course it was stupid. She spends a week here and goes crazy for an old man. She's your garden-variety crackpot—obviously. But why do guys have to be such utter and hopeless pricks? They pretend like they're letting you off gently because they think you just might be that stupid." She paused, then looked at me. "I wanted to come see you in case I didn't get another chance."

"You're going?"

She nodded. "I guess you better make up with your girlfriend," she said. "What's her name again—Rose, right?" I told her it was. "Rose," she repeated, considering it, with a wan smile. She looked so perfectly breezy. I was unhappy to see her go, heartbroken possibly, but I wasn't going to say anything. By remaining silent I hoped to pass myself off as grown-up and sensible, but it was hard being, I hate to say it, brave. "I bet you won't even remember me in two weeks."

She waited for a response, then looked to the ground.

I led her home, my unpresentable, squalid home. Not that I had many qualms about cleanliness, but I admit feeling a twinge of shame as I kicked away a pair of my underwear from the landing of the stairway.

Jana stood reading in the living room when we came in. She put down her magazine, her hands knotted into fists. I introduced her to Marina.

"I'm a friend of Ian's," she said.

"I know." Jana paused. "Saul told me." Jana smiled, her jaw locked, chained and deadbolted, before disappearing into the kitchen. "Would you like some coffee?" she asked. "Or tea? I can make both."

"We're going upstairs, Jana," I said. She gave me a funny look, which I chose to ignore.

We took the twelve lime-green carpeted steps up to my room.

Marina stood by my desk, staring out my window to the complex parking lot and cul-de-sac. My reading lamp was still on.

"Are you writing something?" she asked.

"A letter," I said. I lunged over to the desk, folding three sheets of loose-leaf and putting them in my pocket.

"Man of mystery. I like that."

"It's none of your business," I snapped back, my voice suddenly cracking. "Nothing you'd be interested in."

"I'll take your word."

On my dresser drawer, in matching silver frames, Jana had put some pictures.

She pointed to one school portrait. I was in a T-shirt and pin-striped overalls in front of a blue backdrop.

"How old were you here?"

"I think I was eight."

"You look adorable."

"Thanks."

"And this one?"

"I'm five, I think." I was on a lake in front of a canoe, an orange life jacket engulfing my face. Beside me, a silver-haired man held two fishing poles. "That's my grandfather." Even after my father took custody of me, I would visit my grandparents in the summers until they died.

Marina smiled.

"He's a nice-looking guy."

"I miss him," I said. "He passed away when I was twelve." I thought of him now as I stared at a picture I normally paid little attention to. His stomach would bulge from a short-sleeved cotton shirt, and his slacks were held up by thick red suspenders. He was a barber. I remembered jars of liquid colored blue like sinister potions, in which he'd dip his combs, and his customers, wiry gray men in plaid sweaters who stepped into the shop, the local paper tucked under their arms. Grandfather would hum "Lily of the Valley" as he lathered soap, before putting the straight-edge against their necks. His face was pink, with folds of loose skin that hung from his jaw. He had watery blue eyes. His fingers were stubby—like my dad's—his nails kept short and filed, gray hair on his knuckles. He wore two rings: a gold wedding band and a pinky ring with a blue stone in it.

He had a thick mustache stained yellow from nicotine. I missed his mustache. He would let me play with it after dinner, once he'd had a couple of glasses of Irish whiskey. When I went off to bed, he would kiss me, and his mustache would feel scratchy and his breath would smell of alcohol. I used to stare at the bottle through the glass of the locked liquor cabinet. It was squat like a milk bottle with a stubby neck. The liquid inside it was a faint yellow. And although I didn't read at the time, the label of the bottle read "Bushmills" in gold lettering, the very same drink my father immortalized in 1974.

"Do you know where you're going?" I asked.

"Don't know. Louise thinks she wants to take a term off and keep traveling, though she might change her mind. Actually, it's not so hard getting around and meeting people. We thought Ian was going to be this recluse who lived off in the woods somewhere, like a male version of Helena, drinking malt liquor and collecting child porn, but here he is in a suburb, accessible by public transit. Who knows? I guess we'll go wherever the buses take us. A Romanian dramaturge Louise wrote to finally replied, though we're not planning to go that far." She stopped and bit her thumb. "Can I ask you a question?"

I nodded.

"Are you going to forget about me?"

"I don't think so."

"You don't think so?"

"I mean, no."

"I don't believe you, not a word of it," she said. "You've got better things to do. I've accepted it. Otherwise, I'd ask you to run away with me. There's no hope for me. Don't deny it. I bet if I see you on the street ten years from now, you won't recognize me. I'll be on the street corner busking for my dinner, and you won't even throw one thin dime into my violin case."

She said this sweetly and wistfully. And I figured she was right. She made a violin-bowing gesture with her hands again, just as she did at the doughnut shop, though this time she closed her eyes as if she were in rhapsody. Suddenly she seemed wise. If grace qualified as knowledge, then she was rich in wisdom. I closed my eyes, too, and tried to hear her invisible tune.

I borrowed Jana's car that morning because I was supposed to meet Richard at his hotel, but first I wanted to drop off a letter to Rose. I drove to her part of town, the area in which one cul-de-sac lined with BMWs and SUVs led into another. Crumpled and folded in my inside jacket pocket was the letter. It was written in red ballpoint and took up five single-spaced sides of loose-leaf, torn from a ringed notebook. In it, I asked Rose to forgive me because I didn't love her. I was hardly a prolific letter-writer, but now, when I had only this one thing to say, I was able to take up so much paper.

I had fooled her. I pretended I felt deeply about her so I could
sleep with her, like so many other boys I knew who joked about
doing the same thing with their girlfriends. I never joked about
it and I supposed that was even worse, because I knew better—I
knew what I did was cruel. Mean. Girls called boys "mean," as
in "you're being so mean." Boys couldn't say "mean" without
sounding like babies, without risking their claims to manhood.
That was our only concern. Girls were the ones who had real
worries. They had to actually keep from making babies.

About a block away I could see her stepping out of the passenger side of a car. She was in a trench coat, her hair tied back
in a ponytail. She looked pale and distracted. She looked sick
and I figured she didn't want to see me. I wasn't looking forward to what she might say to me, or what her mother might
say to me. She didn't notice me approaching in the car. She
wobbled as she walked, like she had a cramp. She stopped, put
the heel of her hand to her forehead. Her mother helped her to
the house, leading her by the elbow. Mrs. Clark looked back,
but I was out of sight.

Richard's bed was unmade. His stuff lay fanned atop the motel
television set, on display: his wallet, opened face down, his
loose change and his passport, his tobacco, rolling paper and
four purple Bic lighters. Andreas sat on Richard's bed, speaking
German into the phone. The door was left ajar when I walked
in. Richard sat in a chair changing channels on the TV, dressed
in a white bathrobe and black leather slippers, clicking the
remote, which was bolted down to the night table. He nodded
at me. The bruise on his face was now yellow.

"You are late," he said finally.

"I was busy."

"Andreas and I must leave soon."

I took Richard's cheque from my pocket and held it out for him to take.

"This belongs to you."

Richard waved it away.

"I can't take it."

"Tear it up, then. Flush it down the toilet; keep it," he said. "It is not important. It is not my money, anyway."

Andreas finished his conversation on the phone and said something to Richard.

"It was good meeting you," Andreas said after a pause and a gulp. It was as though he'd swallowed the English language. "I wish you well."

He shook my hand, then stepped out into the hall. Richard asked me to take a seat. I tried to refuse, but he insisted, so I sat across the room in a chair next to a window and a brown air-conditioning unit.

"How do you do?" he asked.

"Fine."

"Fine? You left in a hurry yesterday at the chapel."

"I did."

"I understand. Both my grandmothers died last year. It is hard to see a corpse, yeah?"

I nodded.

"The flowers were shit," he said. "The music was shit. The priest was shit. The speakers were shit."

Richard faced the television, turning to me once and smiling falsely, flashing his gapped teeth, which seemed outlined in brown grime.

"Why are you so sad, Richard?"

"Because death is shit."

He crossed his bare legs and continued flipping channels.

"Do you blame me for her death?" he asked.

"No."

"Thank you." Richard turned off the set. "The news is not what it used to be."

"When do you leave?" I asked.

"This evening we return to Germany. I leave abruptly, this is true. I have spoken to the network. We are no longer with them. They say I have devoted too much time and too much resources on this segment. The profit motive is a priority, of course. It is like this everywhere among the bourgeoisie, so is life. The network suggests I focus on the group Urethra Franklin. They say there are two nine-year-old boys, little fair-headed boys, who will claim one band member fondled them. The network would be interested in that. Already, they have become tired of Helena St. Pierre. They shall air what I have already recorded. This shall suffice, they tell me. Another producer is to edit the piece. I shall not allow them to have it. I have resigned. I shall burn the videotape before I surrender it to them. Maybe Andreas is burning it as we speak." He looked past me for a moment. "This is my promise to you, Saul. I am not a harlot. The piece is important to me. They will not fuck with my piece. They will not fuck with my video footage."

I crossed the room to the door.

I offered the cheque to him, held it as though to rip it up.

"Don't," Richard said, wincing. "Leave it here."

I held out the cheque. He stood and took it, placing it in his front pocket.

"You must keep in contact, Saul. I may need to speak to you in the future. You may wish to speak to me then."

"Sure."

"It is settled."

He sat down on the bed and rolled a cigarette, holding it in his fingers. He asked me to toss him a lighter. I did.

Richard held the lighter in front of his face, the cigarette in his mouth. He put the lighter down.

"I shall quit."

What would my mother think of the throng gathered outside the church? Policemen had set up sawhorse gates to keep them away from the path leading to the church entrance, which they huddled against solemnly. They were mostly men well into middle age. Along with the hate mail and the death threats made from untraceable mobile phones, these very same people had left flowers at my father's door, wrapped in cream-colored paper or in peanut butter jars half filled with water, cards, ones with sappy illustrated kittens addressed to me, pictures ripped out of magazines and pasted onto brown cardboard with "Why?" written in marker underneath, and stuffed animals, pocket-sized white teddy bears. They couldn't get into the church itself, which was already at full capacity, but remained here on guard, marking the area as if it were another St. Pierres concert, snapping photographs and playing "Bushmills Threnody" on small tape recorders, especially now, as former members of the St. Pierres' touring band and Father Felix stood ready to help carry my mother's coffin inside.

The car stopped behind the hearse, the back door of which was already open. The coffin was wheeled to the steps of the church, then lifted up by the pallbearers. What a gorgeous cof-fin, I thought, in spite of myself. The sun was warm against my face. I got out of the car first, followed by Jana and my father.

"This is a fucking nightmare," Dad muttered. Cameras snapped and flashed at him.

"Look at the turnout," Jana said. She almost squealed. "Do you think you'll have as many people at your funeral?"

Dad shot her a dirty look.

I wondered who wouldn't be curious about their own burial. When I was younger, I would imagine watching my funeral from heaven, seeing my father and Jana, my friends and classmates, teachers, in hats and white gloves, clawing at the casket, all of them weeping for me. And then I would see a strange woman emerging from the gaggle of mourners, a woman who would lift her veil and reveal herself to be my mother, her eyes moistening in regret, and this would bring me closer to believing in God. It provided me with an incentive; it provided me with compassion.

Someone asked me to look up at their camera. I raised my head and obliged.

My mother was strange. She had her reasons. She abandoned her own child. She gave herself to God like a drowning man offering himself to the sea.

She gave herself to emptiness.

She gave herself to pavement.

But she might well live forever because there would always be men on this earth who needed their hearts inflamed, men with not a sliver of my father's determination or charm who would like to think they could turn her around. To them, she would remain a sympathetic voice.

They hissed at my father.

Above, in the distance, I could see a dark cloud.

Once in the church's antechamber, the coffin was wheeled in front of the altar. The church was modest and somber, unlike yesterday's chapel with its cream-pink carpet and soft light. It was narrow and stark with whitewashed walls, interrupted by stained glassed windows and a lonely bronze crucifix behind the priest's altar. It smelled of incense, layers of incense old and new, the scent encrusted in the pews and the coffee-colored carpeting. The place seemed almost greasy from it. Another priest, not Father Felix, but an older man with a dark face and droopy eyes, conducted the Mass. The priest led us through the Our Father again. He read from the New Testament. I'd forgotten how participatory Masses could be. We stood up and sat down, we made the sign of the cross, we responded, "Blessed be the Lord." A Mass—heavy, crowded, victimized by gravity. We offered peace to the people seated beside us. I shook my own father's hand halfheartedly and said, "Peace be with you." He mumbled it back to me with menace. The old priest offered communion to those who belonged to the Church, and blessings to everyone else. We, the bereaved family—my father and I, then Jana—were first in line. The priest placed the back of his hand against my cheek, his hound-dog eyes set on my face in sympathy and, though I was never confirmed, placed a communion wafer on my tongue. It felt dry in my mouth and left no taste as I swallowed it.

The graveyard was near full occupancy, I figured. Her grave was at the far corner of the cemetery, away from the chapel and the shade of the older sections with their prim balsams and leafy birches. The plot next to hers was newly filled: soggy wreathes of white daisies still stood huddled crookedly around it. The coffin was lowered by straps into the ground, as more ridiculous hymns were sung and people behind us let out muffled sobs.

My father stood beside me, before an open rectangular hole in the ground, perfectly silent. He hadn't said a word in the car to the cemetery. He looked in pain. Maybe from an ulcer he'd picked up when he first moved to Toronto, which returned during times of stress, or because of the music business and his friends here still in it who remembered the humiliating incident with his first wife, which led to his own early retirement from stardom. Maybe because of the funeral and the money that kept slipping away from him, previously spent by his second wife and his son, someone who utterly lacked any appreciation for him. But then again, he always looked in pain. That was the way fathers looked, like shrapnel was being wrenched from their stomachs, like needles slid underneath their fingernails.

The canopy that had been set up over the grave cast a shadow on his face. He remained calm, even as a man operating an orange crane began to throw dirt into the hole. We watched the hole fill, then the machine operator used the rear side of the crane to pack the dirt into the ground. My mother was being buried, noisily.

The dark cloud in the distance grew.

And then, without warning, my father's eyes flung open and he cried out, surprised, a high-pitched yelp that drew everyone's attention to him.

I recognized her. It was the woman at the doughnut shop. Anders' love object, the reason for his strange threats. She was also the woman who performed "Bushmills" at karaoke night. She had jumped a fence and dodged the policeman running after her. Now she was on my father's back, her press-on fingernails ripping into his face. She was in high heels, a heavy-set woman with a square face and thick arms, a black veil covering her face. There was a bulge in the belt cinching her suit jacket that glinted in the sun—it was a gun. Gord and Father Felix rushed forward and pulled the woman off him. Dad, still howling, spun around and tripped on his own feet, falling to the ground.

"Like the dog you are!" she yelled. "Like the dog you are!"

It happened quickly. With her arm extended and shaking, she assumed a combat stance, lifted the revolver she had wedged into her dress and pointed it at my father, pulling back the hammer. Even though this happened quickly, I remember watching my father's face as I had all day. On it was an expression of serenity. The woman's face was fat and pink with what seemed like gleeful blood lust. Then it appeared as though this confidence had been drained, replaced by a look of confusion and panic— two or three darting glances, a twitch. She swung the gun to her head, set its shiny silver barrel up to her temple, and fired. As she toppled over, her veil came off, her wig came off. This woman was a man. She was another man who loved my mother.

Dad lay sprawled on the ground above my mother's grave, still rubbing his eyes, his face set in a baby's grimace. We could see the back of his mouth. I held out my hand to him. Tears were running down his face as he took it.

I managed to finish high school, after all. Jana rejoiced. This, in spite of the suspension Navi and I were given for the balance of the school year. We took the fall, not for the infamous walkout, which caused no damage, or the toxic nerve gas scare, which we had nothing to do with, but for vandalism, after a man at the hardware store called to report our suspicious behavior with spray paints. Navi's folks were royally pissed off, naturally, even though there was no need to worry. He had already received his acceptance letters and full scholarships from three different universities. Mr. Choi, the principal, brought our parents in and made it sound as if he were doing us a gigantic favor by not expelling us and allowing us to graduate. We were to come to school grounds for our provincials, but to stay off it otherwise. So we ended up studying together at the public library. Navi helped me catch up on a year's worth of English, chemistry and math. I wasn't a bad student after all, not if I sucked it up and did the work.

I attended my graduation ceremony, where I saw Rose for the first time in weeks. She looked happy. I realized I'd never seen her that way, so free of whatever had been bothering her, and it felt as though she was done with me. She seemed to float around in her tacky gabardine graduation gown. I lost track of her on the auditorium stage, but after the last speech was given, she tapped me on the shoulder. She smiled and shook my hand and said she was glad to see me when it was obvious to me she wasn't. Rose had a face incapable of deception. "You look good," I said in a hopeless attempt at flattery.

"I'm fine with how I look," she said a little coldly.

She smiled again, this time without looking in my eyes, then returned to her parents.

Both Jana and my father attended my graduation. Jana took pictures of us in which we all looked happy, almost lighthearted. We went out for dinner with Gord and pregnant Nadine, where, as a graduation present, Dad opened a briefcase and passed across the table a stack of twenty-dollar bills. Trust Dad to part so dramatically with his cash. Ten thousand dollars.

"It's up to you what you do with it," Dad said.

Jana put her hand on mine and nodded in agreement. They were attending weekly counseling sessions.

In August, I took a train across the country, the same trip my mother had made thirty years earlier. I wanted to get to the Maritimes, but after four days without sleep in my second-class seat, I found myself in Toronto. I looked up Nathan Shaw and stayed with him and his wife. Maybe it was the old family charisma, but Mrs. Shaw took to me and said I could stay as long as I wanted. I liked Mrs. Shaw. She was thin, taller than Nathan, with long spindly fingers, dusty-blonde hair and an almost English lilt at the end of her questions that made her sound delicate, maybe brittle. That night, we had something with pheasant and mint for dinner and then retired to the attic porch, where we sipped wine from a bottle that rested on the window ledge next to an air conditioner. This was what my parents had missed out on: it wasn't too bad.

I told Mrs. Shaw I'd never eaten as well at someone's home. She was slumped in a wicker chair, out of which, I would learn later in my stay, it was near impossible to move.

"We eat in all the time," she said, pointing a leftover bread-stick at Nathan, "because he doesn't like lineups. He has panic attacks unless we sit by the window. I would say he has a functional fear of crowds."

"I would say *functional* is a convenient word, isn't it?" he responded.

Mrs. Shaw smirked, shooting a sidelong look at me.

"A funny man, he is. That's why we keep him around."

"I like to think that I'm only being fire conscious," Nathan continued, "more prescient in the arena of disaster. I know a thing or two about human nature. I was, after all, a child of the sixties."

Mrs. Shaw burst out laughing.

She said she was glad to have me here. Both their children, aged twenty-one and nineteen, lived away from home during the school year and were in Europe this summer. They were sisters who got along so poorly that they phoned home every few days to learn the whereabouts of the other to avoid being in the same country.

I was glad to take their hospitality. I said I wanted to spend a week in Toronto, but stayed more than a month. For the first few days, I hung around the house for a while, eating all their peanut butter and Premium Plus crackers, excited about the different TV stations in Ontario. Nathan and I bummed around occasionally. We went to Italian bakeries and watched the women on the street, but even though he was funny and sarcastic, it was still like hanging around someone's parent.

"Have you read my book?" he asked me point-blank one afternoon while we were watching televised rugby.

I nodded. I was about to say something about it, the thing I had prepared to say about it, but he interrupted me.

"I guess I haven't talked much about Helena. It's not as though I've been afraid; it's more as though I don't know where to begin." His face sort of screwed up, this almost oxygen-deficient expression, as he began to mumble. "How's this—I'll write it down."

"Good for you," I said, punching him in the arm. "I'll be in the kitchen if you need any moral support."

I considered calling people I knew in the city. I thought about ringing Leslie Erickson, the man who wrote my parents' biography, the weirdo who spent all of June pestering me about my life story. But I decided to go to the Hockey Hall of Fame, where I stared at hockey memorabilia: international jerseys and historic sticks. The Stanley Cup was out for the summer, but I saw all the other trophies and watched videotaped replays of vicious hockey slashes in the screening room. The entrance to the hall was, like a lot of Toronto, part of an underground mall and led to a food court, where I had a piece of gourmet Thai pizza.

From there I stared at my map and figured out how to get to Yorkville, the neighborhood once composed of narrow, Victorian-style row houses. Back in 1967, there was a riot when the hippies blocked off the streets for three days after a downtown happening was broken up by police. The hippies wanted the street closed to traffic, and the city wanted the area cleaned up and turned into a shopping center. It looked as though the city had won. The brick houses of Yorkville were now upscale boutiques and restaurants. Places like the Riverboat and the Village Corner were rendered obsolete in the seventies after the drinking age was dropped to eighteen. I walked along Bloor Street and tried to imagine my parents here, my dad in his very own army-surplus jacket, ringlets of blond hair covering his face, running into my mother, wispy and quiet, disconcertingly seductive under her soft words. I sat on a bench a block from the subway station, facing the weeds and rubble of an empty lot, and then, at its far end, the front façade of an otherwise demolished building. It looked ancient and ruined.

I would call home. Jana inevitably answered the phone, picking up after the first ring, eager to hear from me.

"Did you hear about the man they arrested for making the threats?" Jana asked. "He had an entire shack, an abandoned barn, where he made real toxic nerve gas. The walls of the shack were covered with pornography."

"Tell me how you are."

"We're doing well," she said. "I've been helping Nadine with her knitting for the baby. She's been poking herself a lot."

I asked about my father, who had been depressed after the funeral. He puttered around with his guitar in the new kitchen, filled with nervous energy, electing not to eat or drink. For once we wanted him to get nice and drunk and let it all out, but he had stopped drinking in the same effortless way he had given up smoking. We watched him shrivel in his newfound sobriety, his clothes falling loosely. Jana pleaded for him to get help, which he did only out of vanity once his hair started falling out in clumps.

"Why don't you have a word with him," Jana suggested. I hesitated, and to fill the silence, she whispered, "He's responded well to the medication."

I heard my father asking to talk, then Jana passing the phone over to him.

"I'm on something," he said, his voice dripping with cheer. "Though being on it makes me forget what it is."

"How are you?"

"I'm surviving, Saul. I talk to a man with a funny Austrian

accent. We've decided that I'm the gloomiest songwriter of my generation. The word he uses is *lebensmüde*."

"Good."

"Are you having a good time?"

"I am."

There was a pause, as though he had reconsidered saying what he wanted to say. "When are you coming back?"

"Before Christmas, I think." I planned to be home for Christmas. Then I would figure out where to go next.

"Excellent. Come back safely. You'll get to meet Dr. Blum at the group session. He happens to be a fan."

I went to a lake an hour away from Toronto. I set up a borrowed tent in a clearing off the beach and sat on a log that day. The water was silver and clear. Was this where my grandfather used to take me? I couldn't remember. Maybe. It was nearly impossible to see the other end. I got back to town and met up with Navi, who was starting his degree at York University. I left Toronto and spent a week in Montreal, where I met a bunch of Australian kids my age, bumming around, like me. I was like any other carefree kid traveling around on someone else's dime. I decided to be that kid—a reasonable facsimile, at the very least—full of drunken goodwill, optimistic and cash-rich, ready to screw if the opportunity arose. I tried very hard to be him.

I visited Marina and Louise in New York and toured museums by myself during the day and played Crazy Eights with them at night. Louise was back at school while attempting to sell her screenplay. She said she was busy stalking Loudon Wainwright III and laughed. Then she kissed the cover of his 1975 album, *Unrequited*, which featured a big picture of

Wainwright, bearded and long-faced, with a glycerin tear running down his cheek.

Marina was working at the mattress warehouse and taking Yiddish lessons. She had dyed her hair black. She was kind enough not to say anything, but I got the sense she was in love with someone. I just knew it. Still, we got along merrily and I slept on their living-room futon alone.

I spent another week in Boston and made my way slowly westward, renting a car in Providence and following road signs until I bought a road atlas somewhere in Ohio. I spent four days in Las Vegas, drinking cheap Corona with off-duty kitchen staff at Circus Circus, before going to see Brice Canyon. I met a woman there, a bartender named Tina whom I nearly slept with, but she kicked me out of her apartment when I made fun of her taste in movies. I drove down to Arizona and spent a night in the desert off an abandoned road. The stars above were pristine, scrubbed of smog and far away from city lights. And the only sounds were of free-range cattle mooing in the distance. I dreamt about how nice it would be to sleep in my own bed. I thought about going home and holding Gord and Nadine's kid, little Helena, and let my eyes close. I dreamt about cooing at little babies, winning their hearts over with my charismatic cooing, as I slept in my rental, a brown Toyota Celica. It only had a radio, so I would listen to AM stations, mostly talk and religious programing, interrupted by an occasional Everly Brothers tune. I began searching along the dial for my parents' songs and only once did I hear them, driving in Utah around sunset, just outside Ogden. It was late November and I had been in the car for hours, long enough not to notice the gorgeous rock formations, slabs of flat mesa, square and craggy and the color of sunburnt flesh. The sky ahead seemed to press the horizon low to the ground and loomed heavy with clouds, sheets of clouds that grew gray in the distance. Off the road were desert scrub and Day-Glo road signs. Then I saw a field of tree stumps, jagged and dark in yellow grass, that sort of resembled a flock of petrified sheep. I had been switching radio stations compulsively, this after drinking cups and cups of coffee. The coffee gave me panic attacks, and I drove with geriatric caution as thoughts of mangled sedans and human splatter crossed my mind. I slowed the car down, drifting toward the gravelly shoulder as I turned the dial. I felt my mother's voice, felt it along the back of my neck, felt my heart pounding from caffeine, and I longed to be home for the very first time in my life. I drove toward the moon rising in the pale light of dusk.

Acknowledgements

First, I'd like to offer thanks to my teachers: Michael Cunningham, Eduardo Machado, Fenton Johnson, Helen Schulman, David Plante.

The following people were indispensable in the writing of the book, all invaluable readers and dear friends: Marika Alzadon, Margret Bollerup, Christina Chiu, Mark Constantinescu, Sara Frank, Darren Hayward, Dave King, Alec Michod, Derek Mitchell, Ken Orchard, Geoff Thompson.

While writing my novel, I consulted the following books for information about Canadian music and culture in the 1960s: John Einarson, *Neil Young: Don't Be Denied: "The Canadian Years"* (Kingston: Quarry Press, 1992); Nicholas Jennings, *Before the Gold Rush: Flashbacks to the Dawn of the Canadian Sound* (Toronto: Viking, 1997); Margaret Trudeau, *Beyond Reason* (New York: Paddington Press, 1979). The German phrases used in my book were found on a website entitled *Dirty Crap to Say in German* (www.eat-germany.net/crap/dirtcrap.htm).

A couple of notes: "Baroque-a-Nova" is the title of a song by Mason Williams that was once found on the jukebox at Helen's Grill (Main and 25th) in Vancouver. The unnamed town the novel is set in is *loosely* based on Ladner, a suburb of Vancouver that I lived in from ages five to twelve, and one I remember fondly, if not completely accurately.

As for the publication process, I would also like to thank my editor, Barbara Berson, my agent, Beverley Slopen, my brother, and my friends Lee Henderson and Steve Galloway for their encouragement, counsel and formidable lunching abilities.